The Xandra: Book 3
Goddess of Life

By
Herbert Grosshans

Published by
Melange Books, LLC
White Bear Lake, MN 55110
www.melange-books.com

ISBN 978-1-61235-013-4

Goddess of Light, The Xandra Book 3 Copyright © 2006, 2011
Herbert Grosshans

Credits
Cover Artist: A. Bratt
Editor: Taylor Evans
Copy: Mae Powers
Format: Mae Powers

The Xandra: Book 3
Goddess of Life
By Herbert Grosshans

A thousand years have passed since Commander Beringer and the Genaar fled into the bowels of the alien space station. Now awake from a cryogenic sleep, their adventure continues back on Nu-Eden.

You can visit Herbert at his blog
http://www.hegro.blogspot.com

The Xandra Trilogy
Seeds of Chaos Book 1 Eden's Gate
Seeds Of Chaos Book 2 Hell's Gate
Stardogs, Book One, Return to Redsky
Stardogs, Book Two, Redemption
Orion—The Hunt
Cliffs of Time

The Xandra: Book 3
Goddess of Life
By Herbert Grosshans

Prologue

A thousand years have passed since Commander Beringer and the Genaar fled into the bowels of the alien space station. When they awaken, they find the tower where Captain Cunningham and other Xandra-Humans had lived, deserted. The Xandra-plant and all the pseudo-humans have been dead for centuries.

Commander Beringer takes a small team down to Nu-Eden, the alien female soldier Starmote, Lt. Wang, and John Lambert on a mission to find out what happened in the thousand years they've spent in cryogenic suspension.

Great changes have taken place on Nu-Eden. When the Xandra discovered that her creations could not propagate on their own, she decided to let the remaining humans live, because she needed the human men to mate with the female Xandra-born to create new offspring.

Humans have flourished on Nu-Eden. Most of the True-Humans hate the creatures of the Xandra.

The Commander and his team rescue a group of Xandra-born Humans from slavers and promise to accompany them to the City. On their journey, they join up with a farmer's family, who is also on its way to the City of the Xandra. They stop to spend the night at the Ballard Farm, only to find out that raiders, who are still occupying the house, have murdered the family. They overcome the raiders with the help of Starmote and execute them.

Viran, a barbarian from one of the islands in the north, is the Great Mother's 'Chosen One'. She has him rescued from certain death by recruiting the services of John Lambert and his shuttle. Two mysterious women, Mirtin and Vienne, are also among the rescued.

Naomi, a Shadow-Angel, has visited Commander Beringer.

Chapter One

The morning air smelled fresh and cool. Strange, how things never seemed as foreboding and gloomy in daylight.

Commander Beringer looked into the cloudless sky, half-expecting to see the shape of a winged girl against the rising alien sun. Scratching his neck, where Naomi bit him to suck his blood, he attempted to recall the feel of her naked body against his, wanted to remember the heat of her alien vagina. However, the harder he tried the more the events of the night seemed to recede, only fragments remained.

The memory of another naked body proved stronger. Thrusting breasts, gleaming red in the light of the moon, blotted out the ghostly memory of the vampire-girl.

Starmote.

She invaded his mind, taunted him.

Her nude body glistened with droplets of water as she rose out of the lake. When he reached out for her, she laughed, turned and ran away. He watched the play of her plump buttocks, reached out…

"Commander, are you alright?"

His eyes flew open, staring unfocused for a second before they fell on Starmote who rode beside him. "I'm fine," he said, shaking his head to clear his mind.

"You are bleeding from your neck again," Starmote said, reached over to wipe the blood away. Then she brought out her little device and held it against the blood on her finger. "Traces of the same venomous substance in your blood, as I suspected." She looked at him with curiosity. "Tell me what you did last night."

"I went for a walk, then I went swimming with you," he answered.

"What happened on that walk?"

"What makes you think anything happened?"

Starmote pocketed her device, glanced at him. "There are two puncture wounds on your neck, Commander, identical to the ones you had yesterday morning. Unless you inflicted those wounds yourself, something or someone did. What happened?"

Beringer stared at the thick black mane of the horse he rode. The face of a girl with black skin and short black hair appeared in front of his eyes, needle-thin fangs gleamed in her open mouth. Then the vision was gone.

"Naomi," he whispered, "her name is Naomi."

"Who is she?"

"I'm not sure," he said. "She sucked my blood."

"A vampire-entity." Starmote said. "They appear at night to drain their victims of their blood. There is usually a joining of bodies involved."

"They only exist in our legends," Beringer said.

"Not only in yours. Ours, too." Starmote removed the device from her pocket again, adjusted some settings, then she leaned over and pressed it against Beringer's neck.

He flinched involuntarily from the sting.

"We call those creatures *Soul-eaters*, most of them are considered evil. They give you great pleasure while devouring your very soul." Starmote gave Beringer a sharp look. "Tell me, did you have sexual intercourse with that creature?"

Whatever she had injected into him seemed to have cleared Beringer's mind. "I don't remember much, but I think so. I don't believe she is evil, though."

"Maybe not. She will seek you out again, and again, and again. Your body will become weaker with every encounter. She will come until she has taken your last drop of blood. She can't help it--that is her nature. I suggest tonight you don't wander around by yourself. Stay with someone."

Beringer grinned. "With you?"

She didn't smile. "If you wish."

He watched her ride toward the front of the wagon train, an attractive figure on her horse. He twisted his body to look back at the riders behind him. They had eleven more horses, enough to give everyone a mount, but some of the Xandra-born women still preferred to walk.

Quirma Ballard, her son Brico, and her daughter Helgie, had joined the caravan. Although wounded badly, Brico would survive. Quirma's husband, Holger Ballard, and a couple of their sons, already went to the City to deliver the harvest, wagons full of wool. The Ballards were raising sheep-like animals.

One of the Xandra-born saw Beringer looking back. She waived, dug her naked heels into her horse's flanks and let it catch up with Beringer.

Reyna.

Her green eyes shone brightly under long dark lashes as she smiled at him. "I missed you last night," she said. Staring at his neck, she gasped. "You were visited by a Shadow-Angel. Did she collect your seed?"

Surprised by her horrified look, he answered, "I believe so."

"Did you drink from her nectar?"

"You mean did I suck her breasts?"

She nodded. "That is what I mean?"

Shaking his head, he said, "I don't remember. I don't think so."

"That is good. Would it be otherwise your soul surely would have been lost." Reyna leaned over, touched his hand. "Tonight you must lie with me, drink from my nectar. That will wipe out what she injected into you. You will be safe." She smiled at him and pulled at the reins to slow down her mount.

Beringer chuckled. He just received the second invitation this morning. Starmote's had been more subtle than Reyna's, but nevertheless, he had read Starmote correctly, he was certain.

It promised to be a good day.

The three wagons ahead of him rumbled over the packed dirt road. As long as it didn't rain, there would be no problem. The sky had cleared and it didn't look like rain in the near future. They were back on the winding road that ran parallel to the river. There were steep cliffs on this side of the river, since the land had increasingly been rising. The river had widened. On the other side lay a flat valley, surrounded by a deep forest. In the distance ahead of them Beringer could see the tall trees of another forest. The lush prairie grass had given way to a shorter, more sparsely growing variety. Small rocks and boulders were strewn across the landscape.

The wagons creaked as the horses strained against their yokes, trying to pull the heavy load up the incline. One of the riders fell back. Berringer recognized Aran, the young man he first spoke to when encountering Esram's family. He smiled at Beringer, let his horse fall in beside him. "My father is a little worried," Aran said. "Robar hasn't come back yet. Father sent him ahead early this morning to scout out the forest. He should have been back by now."

"Maybe he's taking a little nap while waiting for us to catch up," Beringer suggested. "Or maybe he got lost."

Aran shook his head. "Not Robar. He is the best. He can find his way back in the dark. Besides, he took two of the hounds with him."

"Anything I can do?"

Aran smiled. "Father wonders if maybe you, with your strange weapon, could ride up front with him, just in case we encounter some difficulties. There could be bandits ahead."

"Those trees would be a good spot for an ambush," Beringer agreed.

When Beringer reigned in beside Esram, the old man greeted him with a short nod. "I'd like to get into the trees before midday," he said and spit a wad of some black substance into the dust. "There's water there for the horses, and I'm sure the women wouldn't mind taking a dip."

Beringer wiped his forehead. "Neither would I, the sun is suddenly getting hot. I'm not used to this heat."

Esram chuckled. "Wait till that ball of white fire rises higher. This is usually the hottest time of the season."

"Aran tells me you're worried about Robar?"

The old man spit again. Taking something out of his pocket, he shoved it into his mouth. "He should've been back, this is not like him." His voice sounded thick, tired. "This whole business with Ballard's family makes me jumpy and angry. I hope that we'll find Holger and his two sons alive and well in the City."

"Does this kind of thing happen often?" Beringer asked.

"Only for the last couple of years. Never this close to the City."

"Those men, who murdered your neighbors, are they members of an army?"

Esram snorted. "Some army. They call themselves *The Pure-Ones*, those murdering bastards. They're just a bunch of fanatics, who believe everybody is evil, except them. *Satan's Mistress*, that's what they call the Xandra." He laughed, spat a black gob onto the dusty road. "If it weren't for these raids, we wouldn't really need to worry about them too much. They'll never get enough men together to form a real threat. They would never openly declare war against us anyway. They are much too cowardly for that. Most fanatics are. When we get to the City, I'll have a talk with Colonel Bandares, he commands the army that protects the City. Maybe he'll send out a group of soldiers to get rid of the small bands that roam Xandra-land."

Beringer filed away this little bit of new information. An army!

Something began nagging him in the back of his mind. The Pure-Ones, he had heard the name before, he just didn't remember where. "These Pure-Ones, they are a religious group?"

"They pray to some god they call *Odinallah*, a male warrior-god, who does not acknowledge any other gods, especially a female one, like the Mother."

"You mean the *Xandra*?" Beringer asked.

Esram nodded. "She is real. She is a goddess. We pray to her. *Their* god is not real. He exists only in their minds. No god would ever command his people to go out and kill innocent beings, human or Xandra-born. It is a false god, an evil one."

"Much blood has been shed in the name of religion," Beringer agreed. "It is part of humanity's history."

"What god do you pray to?" Esram asked.

Beringer smiled. "No particular one. You might say my god has no name, but I am not an unbeliever. I do believe in a Supreme Being."

"Wait till you meet the Mother. You will know that you are in the presence of a Supreme Being."

Beringer didn't answer. Images of a beautiful woman's body melting into a mass of charred flesh from the heat of a laser-burst flashed in front of his eyes. Had they murdered a goddess that day?

A thousand years in real time, weeks in his own memory, still fresh in his mind.

He wiped his hand across his eyes and looked up into the sky. The Xandra was still alive on this planet. Would she remember that incident? Would she recognize him? If so, how would she treat him?

Looking across the river into the valley, he saw a few thin tendrils of smoke rise into the blue sky. They were too far away to see any details with the naked eye. "Is anyone living in the valley?" he asked Esram.

The old man followed his gaze. "I've never been to that side of the river. But, yes, there is a small settlement over there, mostly fruit-farmers. The valley is very fertile, things grow well there."

They didn't receive any warning. Suddenly armed men surrounded them. They popped out of the grass and appeared from behind large boulders and the few trees that were growing along the side of the road.

Beringer's first instinct compelled him to draw his weapon, but he realized immediately that it would be a futile act. There were at least two dozen, maybe three, whom he could see, all of them armed with rifles. Primitive weapons, but deadly just as well.

One of those rifles was trained at Beringer's head.

"Get off that horse!" the man who held the rifle said with a rasping voice. He wore a long coat, similar to the ones the renegades back at the Ballard-farm had worn. Most of the other men were dressed in the same fashion. A red band that decorated the upper part of his left sleeve set the speaker apart from the others. Obviously, their leader.

Beringer followed the man's orders. Esram cursed beside him, but did the same.

"All of you!" the man commanded.

Beringer felt relieved when he saw Esram's sons sliding off their horses without trying to take a stand. If the attackers had wanted to kill them, they could have done so from their hiding places. The fact, that no one had been killed, proved somehow encouraging.

"What do you want?" Esram demanded.

"What do we want?" the man with the raspy voice said and laughed. "We need your horses and we are confiscating whatever you carry in those wagons." He looked down the road, toward the end of the wagon train. "And we want those Xandra-born creatures."

"Why? So you can murder them?" One of Esram's sons said with a loud voice.

"Watch that tone of yours!" the man rasped. "You cannot murder a thing that has no soul. But don't worry, Xandra-lover, we won't end their pseudo-lives. Since they pretend to be women, we will use them as such." He stared at Beringer. "You," he said, "you don't look like a farmer to me."

"I am a visitor to this land," Beringer said.

"A visitor from where?"

"From far away. Across the water."

The man's eyes narrowed below his bushy eyebrows. "From across the water," he mused. "I think the Colonel will find that very interesting." He looked at the gun on Beringer's hip. "What is that?"

"This is a device to make fire with."

"Show me!"/

Beringer removed the gun from its holster, changed the setting to low and pointed it at a clump of dry grass. A thin, white pencil of light set the grass aflame.

"Give it to me!"

When Beringer handed his weapon over, he let the small power crystal inside the handle drop into his palmed hand. The man aimed it at another clump of grass. Nothing happened.

"You have to press that red button," Beringer told him.

Again, nothing happened.

"It doesn't work for everybody," Beringer explained. "This one only works for me. In my land, they call me *Fire-maker*. Better give it back to me."

"No, I'll keep it. Somehow, I don't believe you. It looks too much like a weapon to me."

While he talked, the other men collected the weapons from Esram and his sons.

"Take the horses," he told the men, "then let's get back to camp." He stared at the two hounds crouching beside the wagon. "Kill the hounds!" he ordered.

Beringer heard Esram's moans when the two animals fell under a volley of bullets. The raiders took no chances with them. No less than five of them emptied their rifles into the large hounds.

The crying of a baby caused Beringer to look to one of the wagons. Esram's daughter, Mirna, clung desperately to her baby-boy while one of the raiders tried to pull the child away from her.

"Leave her alone!" Esram called out hoarsely and stepped forward to help his daughter. The butt of a rifle smashed into his midriff, causing him to double over and gasp for air.

"You don't move, unless I tell you!" rasped the bandit-leader, then to his man, "Let her be."

A couple of rifle shots rang out from the back of the wagon train. When Beringer looked, he saw a man slump to the ground.

Vic, one of the Xandra-born men.

"Damn you!" he bellowed angrily, "there was no need for that." When he stepped away from the group, he heard the crack of another rifle shot. A sudden kick to his left thigh threw him to the ground. He cried out involuntarily as sharp pain ripped through his body. Red stain began coloring his pant leg.

A shadow loomed over him; he looked up to stare into the barrel of a rifle, aimed at his head. "You die now!" The man grinned.

Beringer became aware of the sudden smell of ozone. The grin on the man's face froze and turned it into an ugly mask, decorated with a small red hole between the eyes. The rifle fell from his hands. He crumpled into a lifeless heap.

A figure in combat dress sprang over the dead body, uttering a sharp ear-piercing cry.

Lt. Wang.

Before anybody could react, Wang stood behind the bandit-leader, the shiny blade of his knife against the man's throat. Wang looked at the ring of rifles pointing at him. "He's dead before any of you can pull the trigger," he said calmly.

"Put down your weapons," the leader spoke with suppressed anger. His men followed his order with reluctance.

Beringer gritted his teeth. The pain started to become almost unbearable. He knew he was losing blood. He also knew that they were dead the moment Wang let the man go. The bandit-leader had been humiliated in front of his men. He could not let it go unpunished.

"Release me," the leader said to Wang.

"I want insurance that nobody gets hurt," the lieutenant said.

"You have it."

Wang chuckled grimly. "Are you a man of honor?"

Before he received an answer, the slim figure of a girl rushed to Beringer's side, knelt beside him. "Are you alright, Beringer?" she asked, her green eyes large with concern.

Beringer nodded, smiled. "Thank you, Reyna. I'm still alive."

Reyna looked at the bandit-leader. "You are lucky," she said loudly. "Beringer is a messenger from the sky-gods. He can kill with lightning bolts from his hands. I will ask him to let you live, if you allow me to look at his wound."

Beringer made the effort to grin. Looking at the bandit-leader, he said, "She is right, you know. I could have killed you, but I came here in peace."

The leader grunted. "There will be no more bloodshed. I promise."

Beringer nodded toward Wang, who let go of his prisoners. Beringer saw Wang slide his knife into his boot, where it became part of the boot's design.

The bandit-leader rubbed his throat. "Tend to his wound," he told Reyna.

The Xandra-girl opened the Commander's belt, pulled down his trousers. Beringer grimaced at her. "Under different circumstances I would say you are quite bold, young lady," he whispered.

Reyna said nothing, just looked at him gravely with her large green eyes.

"I knew you were no simple farmer," the bandit-leader said and threw a thoughtful glance at Lt. Wang. "Your man risked his life for you. I wish my men were that loyal."

Chapter Two

The camp lay on the other side of the hill. Beringer had to upgrade his estimation of their captors. These men were no simple bandits; they were soldiers, members of an army. He counted dozens and dozens of tents strewn haphazardly throughout the valley. Most of them were small, just large enough to house possibly six people. He had no problem recognizing the headquarters. A huge tent sprawled in the center of a large cleared area. Fifty people would easily fit inside.

Beringer sat on the front seat of the lead-wagon, beside Mirna, Esram's daughter. She clutched her baby to her breast, while Beringer held the reins that controlled the horses.

When Mirna saw the tents, a sob escaped her lips. "They are going to use us women like the animals they are," she whispered fiercely. "We should have fought them!"

"And we'd all be dead, including your little boy," Beringer countered, but agreed silently with her. Hundreds of men, most of them probably young, away from female companionship for who knows how long. These women would be a welcome diversion.

They headed for the large empty area around the big tent. As most of the soldiers dispersed, the captives were herded toward the tent and told to sit down.

Beringer flinched when he slowly climbed down from the wagon. Even though he injected himself with painkillers, his leg still hurt when he put weight on it. Reyna had done an excellent job bandaging the wound after Beringer sprayed it with a thin film of blood-clogging *tempskin.*

He turned to help Mirna with her child, but she jumped down unaided, still clutching her child to her bosom.

The tent-flap opened and an older man dressed in a long black cloak stepped out. Thick gray eyebrows shaded his eyes. They rested for a moment on Beringer, and then he looked over the rest of the prisoners. "Farmers and Xandra-born," he said with a rumbling voice and glared at the man with the red beard. "Did you have to kill anyone, Corpo Tivek?" His voice dripped with contempt.

"One of my men shot two of them, but they were wounded and useless." Tivek saluted sloppily.

The older man pointed a finger at Beringer. "That man looks like he is wounded. Why didn't you finish him off?"

"The other two were Xandra-born, General. This man is human-- and he is a stranger. I was told to keep a lookout for strangers." He stepped closer to the older man and handed him Beringer's laser-pistol. "He had this on him; it is some kind of fire-starter, so he claims."

The General took the gun, turned it over, and pressed the firing-stud. When nothing happened, he looked at Beringer. "You," he said, "come here and show me how it works."

Beringer limped over to the General, took the laser from his hand and made a show of pressing the red button at the top of the grip. "It worked before," he said and shook his head. "The fuel supply is probably exhausted. These things are not very reliable." He made a motion to put the weapon back into his own holster, but the old man stopped him.

"Not so fast! I will show this to my adviser. In fact, I want him to see you. Your wear strange, unfamiliar clothes." He turned toward Corpo Tivek. "Take him in for interrogation, and take this with you."

Tivek pushed Beringer toward the entrance of the tent and then through it. As soon as Beringer stepped into the tent, he became aware of a musky old-leather-smell assaulting his nostrils. When his eyes adjusted to the gloomy interior, he noticed the curtains hanging from the ceiling. They divided the big tent into a number of smaller rooms.

Beringer met his interrogator in one of the rooms. A tall man, his age hard to determine behind his neatly trimmed beard. He didn't seem at all like the savage looking bunch Beringer met so far. Dressed in a tight-fitting black bodysuit, the play of corded muscles, visible beneath the thin material, made the man's physical condition clearly evident. Although his face looked gaunt, his body wasn't. The play of corded muscles was clearly visible underneath the thin material.

When Beringer looked into his dark eyes, alarm bells went off inside his head. This man could be dangerous.

He was not a native of this planet!

A small opening in one of the walls brought light and fresh air into the small room. It also illuminated the golden buckle on the man's belt. It depicted the symbol of the atom inside a starburst. The long thin rod strapped to the belt could be nothing else but a weapon--and not one that shot bullets.

Corpo Tivek handed the man Beringer's gun. "I took this fire starter from the prisoner, Colonel. The General wants you to look at it, and he wants you to interrogate the prisoner."

The man took the weapon, turned it over in his hands. His dark eyes rested on Beringer. "A fire starter," he said dryly, his voice deep and resonant. He waved at Tivek. "Leave us! I want to be alone with the prisoner."

Tivek bowed and backed out of the room. The black-clad man looked after him and murmured, "Imbecile." Then he turned back toward Beringer. "I am Massater," he said. "What are you doing on this planet?"

Beringer smiled. "I could ask you the same question?"

Massater chuckled. "I am not the prisoner here." He gestured toward a small leather-covered bench. "Have a seat. By the way, you can speak freely. I keep a damper-field around this room."

Beringer sat down, gratefully. "Thank you." He could feel his thigh throbbing dully.

"I know this is a weapon," Massater said. "I've never seen one like it. Looks like an antique laser-gun."

"Antique!" It was Beringer's turn to chuckle. "And they told us it was the latest and best military hardware available." *A thousand years ago it probably was,* he reminded himself. *Now it is antique, like everything else about me.*

"Your uniform," Massater broke into his thoughts. "It does not look familiar."

"Neither does yours," Beringer countered. What should he tell this man?

Massater shook his head. "You must surely come from some backwater planet if you don't recognize the uniform of the *Alliance Peace-keepers*. You *are* from off-planet, aren't you?"

Beringer nodded. "I am, but you may have a problem believing the rest of it."

"A year ago, I might have. But now, after spending a year on this god-forsaken place, I am inclined to believe anything."

"Before I trust you with any information, tell me what is your connection with these people here. The General called you his *Adviser.* Is this a regular army or just a band of renegades?"

"It's an army, from Amaar."

"Amaar? Forgive my ignorance, but I am not familiar with that location."

Massater nodded thoughtfully. "What do you know?" he asked.

Beringer lifter his hands. "Not much. I've been here only for a few days. Not enough time to learn anything."

"Amaar is the country to the north. The people there do not believe in the Xandra. A year ago, just about the time when I arrived here, a group of fanatics, The Pure-Ones, took power. Their leader, who calls himself The Reverend, claims to be the descendent of a man named Reverend Champain. He declared a Holy War against the Evil Mistress of Satan and her spawn."

"Reverend Champain," Beringer mused. "I've heard that name before. He was with Beta-Colony, if I'm not mistaken."

Massater looked at him sharply. "Did you say Beta-Colony? How would you know about that?"

Beringer sighed. "Beta-Colony was one of the sites the original settlers built on this planet. The other one was Alpha-Colony. All of the colonists were absorbed by the entity known as Xandra and then recreated. As far as I know, there were no survivors."

"How long ago was that?"

"A thousand years for you, for me only months."

"I don't understand."

Beringer leaned forward, winced, when he became aware of his leg wound. Through the small opening in the wall, he saw dark clouds gathering in the blue sky. How he longed to be back in the safety of a ship, where the viewing screen displayed the blackness of space, instead of wide-open sky.

"My job was to protect the colonists in space, not on the surface of a planet. I am a space-marine, trained to push buttons, fight images on a screen, not a real, solid enemy." When he saw the other man's blank look, he smiled. "I was supposed to be back on Earth in five years. It didn't work out that way. Instead, I am here, sitting in a stinking tent, a bullet wound in my leg. A prisoner. A thousand years later."

Massater's eyes widened. "Are you telling me you came here a thousand years ago? What happened?"

"We went into cryogenic suspension."

"But that's impossible. Earth didn't have the technology back then. Even now, we can keep somebody frozen only for a maximum of a hundred years, and that is risky."

"We found an ally." Beringer said.

"Are you talking about that huge black sphere up there circling this planet?" Massater asked.

Beringer nodded.

"But that's a dead relic. Evidence of life inside was never found."

"We were dead, alright, frozen. For a thousand years." Beringer looked at Massater. "What do you know about Beta-Colony?"

Massater shrugged. "There is a holy site in Amaar, they call it Betacoly. I've been there, and I was puzzled by the ruins I saw."

"If it is anything like the Alpha-Colony site, then I know what you found."

"The buildings were mostly decayed, nothing more than rusted metal and clay walls, overgrown with moss and slimy vegetation, inhabited by what passes for rodents on this planet. The structures were spartan, functional, like military barracks, almost."

"Materials brought down from the colony-ship."

"Now it all makes sense," Massater said slowly, his eyes rested thoughtfully on Beringer. "A thousand years is a long time, things change. Those huge colony-ships that traveled for decades on missions to find suitable planets, carrying thousands of frozen colonists are a thing of the past. Our Dive-Ships cross the emptiness of space from here to the Solar System in two months, maybe less. Unfortunately, most records of the early exploration days are lost. There were wars, you know. The world you remember does not exist anymore. The military power you served is long gone. What was your rank?"

Beringer smiled thinly and made a mock-bow. "Forgive me for not introducing myself. I am Commander Les Beringer of the Terran Space-Navy."

"The Terran Space-Navy." Massater chuckled. "Like I said, there were wars. The balance of power has shifted. Earth is not one of the super-powers. Powerful? Yes, but no match against the *Alliance* and the *Mandarin Empire*. Remind me to brush you up on your history one day, Les."

Beringer grimaced. The other man had not used his rank, had in fact addressed him by his first name. Only Captain Cunningham had done that, but they had been friends. Did Massater try to create a friendly atmosphere? Why? "So, what role are you playing in this so-called Holy War?" he asked.

Massater's face showed no expression. "I am an observer, that's all. I was sent here to gather information. After one year I still don't know anything of real importance."

"It seems to me that you know more than you admit. For one thing, the people you are associated with, these *Pure-Ones*, they are committing genocide on a large scale." Beringer spoke more sharply than he had intended.

"There is nothing I can do about that. My position here is quite precarious, I may be an advisor to the Great General Rodriguez, but I am absolutely without power. So, don't judge me, Beringer."

Beringer shifted in his seat, reminded again of his injury. "What is going to happen to the people who were captured with me?"

"Are they human?"

"Some of them. Simple farmers, from what I saw. There are Xandra-born women."

"The soldiers have been away from their women for a long time. These Xandra-born love sex, you must be aware of that. No harm will come to them."

Beringer laughed dryly. "Rape is considered a harmless activity, is it?"

"They will be willing participants, believe me. The Xandra-born are not human, even if they appear to be. Their thought processes are alien to us."

Beringer fell silent. He had no answer to that. Massater was right, the Xandra-born were alien. How alien? He didn't know. He remembered Vic and Torka, the Xandra-born men. "They murdered two of the males in cold blood, just because they were not human. They were men, as far as I'm concerned, gentle and without malice, not monsters."

Massater shrugged. "It is not my position to pass judgment. I will file my report and let my superiors decide." He looked at Beringer's laser, which he still held in his hand. "Here," he held it out toward the Commander. "You may need this when you try to escape. I know you will try."

Beringer took the weapon, somewhat surprised. "What makes you think I won't use it against you?"

"I wouldn't advise it. The damper field will render any weapon useless. Especially a relic like yours."

"And yours?"

"Even mine." Massater smiled, respect in his dark eyes. "You could be a dangerous enemy, Commander Beringer. But also a valuable friend. I prefer the latter."

Chapter Three

They used the wagons to form a circle and put the women inside. A couple of soldiers, who walked slowly around the makeshift prison, guarded them. Esram and his sons were kept in a tent by themselves, Beringer and Lt. Wang in another, with an armed guard by the entrance.

"They are certainly not very organized," Wang commented in a low voice. "We still have our weapons, we could easily escape."

"We could, just the two of us, I suppose. But we could never free the others. And we'd have to leave the wagons and horses behind." Beringer took a small sip from his canteen. "At least they left us our provisions. By the way, did you see Starmote?"

Wang shook his head. "Now that you mention it, I don't remember seeing her."

"Do you think she might have escaped?" He jerked his head, startled, when he heard the voice.

"Commander, I assume you are alone with Wang?"

"Starmote?" he whispered fiercely. "Where the hell are you? Can you hear me?"

He heard her chuckle inside his head. "I can hear you quite clearly, Commander."

"Are you in the compound?"

"No. I was never captured. I had to make a quick decision. As soon as I saw you give yourself up I got away from there fast."

"Where are you?"

"Not far. Sorry, Commander, there is no time to explain anything now in detail. The translating device behind your ear is more than just that. I have listened in on your conversation with the man named Massater. Is he a friend or an enemy?"

"I'm not sure. He gave me back my gun." Beringer swallowed hard. "What do you mean by *you've listened in*? Can you read my thoughts, too?"

She chuckled again. "No, I can't do that. You have to vocalize if you want to tell me something. But I can hear what you hear. I apologize for the invasion of your privacy, I know it is important to you humans, but this is an extreme situation. You are a soldier, Commander, so you should understand. Hurt feelings and regards for privacy have no place here."

"You are correct about that, except, I wonder, as I've wondered before, what else are you hiding from us?"

She became silent for a moment, then she said, "We are allies, Commander Beringer, but I have my orders. Let me say just this, Starfinder and I will never betray our friendship."

"That is very comforting," Beringer said dryly. "How long have you had me under surveillance?"

"Since you've been captured."

Lt. Wang had been watching the Commander, perplexed, at first, then with sudden understanding. "Are you talking to Starmote?" he asked with a low voice.

Beringer nodded.

"Tell Wang not to worry," Starmote said. "His privacy is still intact. I will speak to you later, Commander."

"Wait, how…?" Beringer listened for an answer, but encountered only silence. "Dammit!" he cursed, wondering if she monitored him constantly or only at certain times. "Starmote," he called, feeling foolish when only silence greeted him.

"How can she communicate with you?" Lt. Wang asked.

"Through that little marvel they put into our skulls," Beringer said, and chuckled when Wang touched his ear. "Starmote said for you not to worry, you still have your privacy."

"I am really relieved," Wang said with a smile. "But from now on I will always be wondering if I'm still alone or if someone is listening in?"

"When we get back to the station, I will have Starfinder explain to me how we can shut this thing off if we want to," Beringer said grimly. "We don't really know anything about the Genaar. They know much more about us Humans from the data-blocks they removed in Captain Cunningham's quarters. I hope we are not wrong about our new friends."

He didn't know if Starmote could hear what he said, but somehow he didn't care, f acing the problem how to get out of here. "There isn't anything we can do at this moment," he told Lt. Wang. "Might as well catch some sleep."

Strange dreams haunted Beringer's sleep. He awoke in the middle of the night, feeling the sudden need to urinate. Sticking his head out of the tent entrance, he found the guard slumped over, snoring loudly. He crawled out of the tent, walked over to a small clump of bushes. Clouds obscured the sky, filtering the light of the two moons.

He looked over to the circle of wagons, didn't see any guards. It should be relatively easy to escape, except, how far would they get? They'd never be able to take the wagons and horses.

A rustling sound in the bushes made him twist around. The quick motion put strain on his wounded leg; he suppressed the urge to cry out when a sudden pain shot through his body.

A dark shadow rose up beside him.

"*It is I, Commander*," said a voice. He realized she had spoken inside his head.

"Starmote, what-the-hell!" Beringer cursed softly. "You almost gave me a heart attack."

"Sorry," she whispered and stepped closer. She looked down at his thigh. "Are you alright? How is your leg?"

"I am in pain," he answered. "But I guess I was still lucky. It is only a flesh wound. That slug could have shattered my bone."

"Let me have a look at it."

Beringer scanned the area, saw no guards. "How did you get this far into the camp?" he asked.

Starmote chuckled. "The guards are not very alert. I have to admit, though, I helped them a little to fall asleep."

"I did find it strange when I discovered our guard sleeping so deeply."

"Let's go into your tent," Starmote suggested. "Just in case somebody wakes up."

They found the guard was still snoring loudly. Starmote followed Beringer through the narrow entrance. Lt. Wang sat up abruptly when Starmote switched on a small light.

"Hello, Wang," Starmote said, smiling.

"What are you doing here?" Wang asked, instantly alert.

"Checking the Commander's wound. Hold this light for me." She removed her backpack and pulled out a small device. "Pull down your pants, Commander."

Beringer grinned. "This is the second time I'm taking off my pants for a woman without having sex."

"At least you didn't loose your sense of humor." Starmote probed the wound with her fingers.

"Easy," Beringer murmured, and moaned. "That hurts."

"Did you take anything for the pain?"

"I did, but it must be wearing off. How does it look?"

Starmote scanned his thigh with her device. "I detect small fibers imbedded in the wound, probably from your pants. They were trapped when you applied the artificial skin. I have to remove it; otherwise you might get an infection."

She held the device against his thigh. Beringer felt a prickling sensation, and then the pain suddenly disappeared. With deft fingers, Starmote peeled off the thin film of pseudo-skin, then she trickled some liquid from a small vial into the wound. Looking at a tiny screen on her device, she proceeded to poke around on his leg.

"I can only repair so much of the damaged area. There will be scarred tissue," Starmote said, "but after this you will heal quickly." She applied a small patch of some transparent material over the wound, moved her device slowly across it.

Beringer watched the patch expand, flow over the injured spot, and soon the wound became almost invisible.

Starmote put her things back into her pack. "It is sealed now," she said, running her fingers over his thigh, a little longer than necessary, or so it seemed to Beringer. She looked at him, her eyes hidden in the shadow of the small light. "You should have no more pain," she said with a low voice.

Beringer moved his leg, surprised to discover he could do so without discomfort. "You're quite some medic," he said and pulled up his pants. Then he grinned at her. "Too bad you can't repair the holes in my pants."

"I could do that, too, if need be, but there is no time for that." Starmote sat on the floor, crossed her legs in front of her, then she took the small light from Wang, shut it off. "Someone might see the glow from the outside," she said in the sudden darkness.

"It's all quiet out there," Wang said. "How did you get past the guards?"

Starmote made a snorting sound. "Even awake they would have presented no obstacle for me." She sounded almost disgusted.

"We could walk right out of here," Beringer suggested.

"We could," Starmote said. "But what about the others? We can't just leave them here?"

"I know, I already thought about that."

"Have you had any luck contacting Lambert?" Starmote asked.

"No, I haven't." He hesitated. "He's got one of your devices in his head. Can you find him with that?"

"Yes, I could. But maybe you should try yourself, again," she suggested. "I prefer not to use my device."

Beringer knew she wouldn't explain any further and didn't press her. He spoke the code words that activated the shuttle's call-number and it surprised him when Lambert answered. "What the hell happened to you, Lambert?" Beringer sounded angry, but he breathed a sigh of relief when he heard Lambert's voice.

"Sorry, sir," Lambert said calmly. "I was detained."

"Detained!?" Beringer snapped. "What do you mean by that? You had orders not to leave your post!"

"I know, sir, and I apologize. But circumstances beyond my control forced me to move the shuttle."

"What? Are you telling me you are not at the landing site anymore?"

"No, sir, Commander. I had to go on a rescue-mission. But everything is under control."

Beringer breathed deeply, then he asked with a calm voice. "Are you a free agent, marine, or are you acting under duress?"

Lambert chuckled. "If you are asking if I'm a prisoner, the answer is no. I am free to go anywhere you tell me to. Ready for your orders, Commander. I have located your position."

Letting out his breath slowly, Beringer said, "Stand by and wait for my orders, Lambert. You may have to move fast. End transmission."

The connection terminated. Beringer stared at Starmote's shadowy form. "He seems alright. I wonder what happened. He is a good soldier; he would never have left his post without a good reason."

Starmote didn't say anything, but Lt. Wang broke the silence. "Do you have a plan, Commander?" he asked.

"I'm not sure. There is enough firepower on the shuttle to wipe out this whole company of so-called soldiers. But I'd like to avoid any unnecessary deaths. Any suggestions?"

"This is a primitive society. People at this level are also quite superstitious. I assume that humans are no different," Starmote said quietly.

Beringer gave a short laugh. "Humans have always been superstitious. You wouldn't believe the many different religions that exist on Earth."

"Who do these people worship?"

"Some god they call *Odinallah*, a God of War."

"Do you want me to handle this?" Starmote asked.

"What do you have in mind?"

"Just tell Lambert to meet me close to the camp before dawn."

"Alright." Beringer nodded in the darkness. As soon as Starmote had left the tent, he contacted Lambert, gave him his orders, then he settled down to catch some sleep.

Something woke him up. He felt the urge to go outside, again. Quietly he slipped out of the tent. The guard still slept. Walking back to the clump of shrubbery where Starmote had surprised him, he stood, looked with uncertainty around him.

"I watched your friend leave," said a soft feminine voice from the shadows. "Why didn't you go with her?" Her voice triggered something in his brain. "Naomi?" he asked, staring into the darkness of the shrubs. She stepped forward. He could barely see her.

"You are a prisoner," she stated, "but you need not be. I can take you with me right now."

He shook his head. "It is not that easy. I can't leave my friends." Memory of being with her flooded back into his mind. He also remembered Starmote's words. "I was warned against you and your kind," he said.

Naomi laughed softly. "Humans tell many stories about my kind. Not all are true."

She came closer and touched his face. The heat from her hand traveled through his body. It felt like the touch of an electric rod. "I burn for you, Human Beringer, and I can feel that you burn for my touch, also," she whispered and began to undo his belt.

He groaned and let her push down his pants. She touched his growing erection, laughed and pushed him onto his back. Just a foggy shadow against the dark sky, she squatted above him. Sinking slowly into his lap, she sucked his hard organ into her alien vagina and sat without moving for a while, only her inner muscles milking him gently. Then she began to rotate her hips with slow, gentle movements.

"We have time," she whispered above him. "There is much night left."

He closed his eyes, just concentrated on the pleasure that pulsated through his body.

Chapter Four

Beringer awoke and looked around, momentarily disoriented. Scratching his neck absentmindedly, he noticed Lt. Wang gone. He h ad no clear memory of the night. Images flooded his mind. *A dark, winged female figure looming above him. A naked breast, a thick nipple held to his lips. The taste of a sweet, musky liquid. The thrust of hot loins against his.* These things could not have been figments of his imagination.

When he saw the tiny droplets of blood on his fingers, he became certain. Naomi, the Shadow-Angel, had paid him another visit.

The flap to his tent stood open. He stared at the broad back of someone squatting outside. Sitting up, he felt a wave of nausea and weakness and shook his head to clear it. Rummaging through his backpack, he found a vial of energy capsules, pushed one into his mouth. Biting down, he swallowed the bitter gel. After that, he felt better, but not great.

It must be early morning, he thought. Dim light spilled in through the open tent-flap. He heard voices. Recognizing Wang's voice, he stuck his head through the opening. The guard squatting outside rose to his feet and stepped aside when Beringer crawled out of the tent.

"Good morning, Commander," Wang greeted him.

Beringer looked up into the overcast sky. "Looks like rain," he said.

"How is your leg?" Wang asked.

Beringer had forgotten about his injury. Moving around, he realized that the pain had disappeared. He suddenly remembered Starmote. She had been in their tent, had tended to the wound in his thigh.

"Are you feeling alright, Commander?" The lieutenant asked with a concerned voice.

Beringer turned away so Wang couldn't see his neck. "I'll be fine, just a little groggy, that's all."

Wang looked at the guard who stood watching them, his primitive rifle casually in his hands. "You must be tired, standing guard all night," Wang said to him.

"I am quite alert." The guard's eyes shifted uneasily. He stared at Beringer's neck. "You look sick," he said. "There is blood on your neck."

"It is nothing, just a scratch." Beringer answered.

The guard came closer. "Let me see." He stepped away from Beringer, his eyes wide. "As I suspected. You have been bitten by a Shadow-Angel."

"How can that happen?" Wang asked. "I thought you stood guard all night?"

"I did, but a Shadow-Angel can walk right by you, without you seeing her. She is a creature of the night." He moved his left hand in a circle over his heart. "Shadow-Angels are evil creatures. They come at night, when you sleep. You cannot resist them. They copulate with you, give you great pleasures. But you pay. They take your blood and your soul." His voice dropped to a hoarse whisper. "You see, they are creatures of the Xandra and they possess no soul of their own, just like all of the other Xandra-born. Shadow-Angels take a little bit of your soul every time they come to you. That is how they stay alive."

"Superstition," Wang said.

"Not superstition," the guard protested and pulled aside the collar of his coat. Both Beringer and Wang stared at the series of small puncture marks on the man's neck. "I was lucky," the guard said and covered the scars. "My brother came upon us as I lay with one of them. He killed the foul thing with a metal tipped spear, the only way to kill them."

Beringer shook his head. Naomi's lovely face and body suddenly clear in his mind's eye. How could a beautiful creature like that be evil? He didn't believe in mystical beings, or evil demons. Admittedly, there were things on this planet that defied logic. This was an alien world. Things like that had to be expected, but everything had a logical explanation.

"Commander!"

The voice cut into his thoughts, startling him. Looking around, he realized that it had come from inside his head.

"I'm going to answer the call of nature," Beringer said aloud, looking at the guard. The man nodded and said, "Don't wander too far. I'm supposed to watch you."

Beringer walked toward the clump of tall shrubs that he remembered from the night before. "Starmote," he said with a low voice. "Where are you?"

"I'm in the Lander, with Lambert," Starmote answered. "We are close by and ready."

"What are you planning?"

"A show. These people are about to be visited by a goddess."

"I hope you know what you are doing. I want no violence."

"No violence, Commander. At least not from us."

Beringer looked around the campsite. There were small fires everywhere in front of the tents, with soldiers squatting around them. The air felt damp and chilly, Beringer could see the vapor of his breath. He inhaled deeply, his lungs filled with the strong and nauseating reek of smoke and roasting meat. It made him choke and cough. He had never liked meat for breakfast.

"Everything under control, Commander?" Starmote asked. Beringer coughed and gasped for breath. Then he straightened out, fought the wave of nausea. "Yes, everything is under control." He saw Massater coming out of the big tent. "Go ahead," he told Starmote. "This is as good a time as any."

He walked back to where Wang and the guard were standing, watching him.

"You don't look good," the guard said. "Maybe you'd like our doctor have a look at you?"

Beringer waved him off. "Maybe later." He watched Massater come closer.

"I trust you had a good rest," Massater said and gave Beringer a scrutinizing look. "Are you not well?" he asked.

Beringer shrugged. "It'll pass. Must be the air or something I ate."

"It was a Shadow-Angel," the guard spoke up.

Massater looked at the guard with a dubious expression, then back at Beringer. "They see shadows and monsters everywhere," he said in a low voice.

"And you don't?"

Massater laughed. "I don't believe in legends or fairytales. Or any gods, for that matter. I am a scientist and I believe only in things that I can explain."

"I have seen things that cannot be explained by logic or reason," Beringer smiled.

As if on cue, he heard someone shout. Looking up, he saw the disk of the shuttle float above the treetops. It came closer, descended and hovered above the empty space in front of the large tent.

"What the hell is going on?" Massater cursed, looking at Beringer. "Are those your people?"

The sudden rage in the man's voice surprised Beringer.

Massater stepped closer. "You should know that this is a closed system. No open contact with the population is allowed until we know what exactly is going on here," he said with an urgent voice.

Beringer looked at him coldly. "I have no such restrictions. As a matter of fact, I have a pretty good idea of what is going on, and so do you."

The shuttle touched the ground. Beringer saw General Rodriguez step out of the tent. The General stared at the foreign object looming in front of him, then he gave some orders to the group of soldiers who guarded the women inside the circle of wagons. The men formed a line, raised their weapons and aimed them at the intruder.

The entrance to the shuttle slid open, the landing gear telescoped down. At first, nothing happened, then a figure appeared in the opening. Even Beringer sucked in his breath and stared at the unexpected sight.

A woman. Naked. Only her breasts were partially covered with small star-shaped patches, barely large enough to hide her nipples. A golden triangle hid her genitals. Around her narrow waist circled a thin iridescent shimmering band, smaller ringlets of the same material adorned her wrists, and from her shoulders cascaded a transparent cape. A golden hood covered her head, leaving only slits for her eyes.

"I am Athena, the Sky-Goddess." Her voice rang clearly across the compound, amplified by the shuttle's speakers.

Beringer recognized Starmote's voice. *Athena*, he thought. *Where in hell did she come up with that name? She knows nothing about Earth-mythologies.*

"I want you to release the prisoners you are holding." Starmote made a sweeping gesture toward the circle of wagons. "I want you to let them leave with all their belongings."

Beringer heard a barking laugh. He realized it came from General Rodriguez. "*The Sky-Goddess,*" the General rumbled and laughed again. "You never seem to amaze me, *Demon-Bride*. I will not be seduced by your appearance, and neither will my men. We pray to only one God, his name is *Odinallah*. You are an abomination, not a goddess. Kill her!" The last words he screamed at his men.

A volley of shots rang out.

Beringer moved forward involuntarily, cursing with a loud, bellowing voice. In the shuttle's doorway Starmote stood, apparently unharmed. She moved her hands, plucked some objects out of the air in front of her, threw them onto the ground. Then she laughed. Pointing a slim hand at General Rodriguez, she said, "Your puny weapons cannot harm me, General. I am immortal, invincible. I am a true Goddess. Your god Odinallah is a false god; he cannot protect you from my wrath. Do not provoke me!"

She climbed down the stairs, stepped onto the ground. Behind her another figure appeared. Another woman, dressed in black, shiny armor. Only her face, arms, and legs were bare. Instead of using the short flight of stairs, she launched herself into the air. A pair of large wings opened like a silvery cloak behind her. Slowly she floated to the ground. Folding her wings she stood wide-legged, looked around.

"I am known as Angela," she said with a clear, loud voice, "and I have a message from the Mother of Light."

"I knew the Xandra had her hand in this. I will not be intimidated!" bellowed General Rodriguez. He ran toward Angela, lifted his rifle.

Starmote raised her hand, from her forefinger flashed a lightening bolt; it hit the General in the chest. The force from the bolt threw him backwards. He collapsed and lay on the ground in a lifeless heap. His rifle discharged as he fell. Somewhere nearby a man screamed.

"This has gone too far," Massater whispered hoarsely beside Beringer. "Stop this charade!"

"If I do that, there will be a bloodbath," Beringer said calmly and added a warning, "don't interfere!"

One of the soldiers bent over the fallen general. He looked up and shook his head. "He is dead," he announced and looked accusingly at Starmote. "The Xandra has never killed before."

"I am not the Xandra," Starmote said. "I warned him. He was a fool." She lifted her hand above her head. "I want you to listen to the Xandra's message."

Beringer looked around him. Groups of soldiers were gathering everywhere. There were not as many as he had first thought. The way they milled around he knew there wasn't much discipline in this army. Now, with the General dead, who knew what might happen. Some of the soldiers carried their rifles; most of them seemed unarmed.

Beringer touched his gun, satisfied with the feeling of assurance it gave him. Out of the corner of his eye, he saw Lt. Wang do the same.

"The Great Mother has grown tired of watching you murder her sons and daughters." The winged girl looked around as she spoke. Beringer felt himself drawn to her like a moth to the flame. Her voice and eyes held him in a hypnotic spell. She had called herself Angela, a name quite fitting. He couldn't take his eyes of her beautiful angelic face. She reminded him of another winged girl, also exceptionally beautiful.

Naomi, the Shadow-Angel with black, shiny skin, sensuous full lips, needle-thin fangs. Beautiful and possibly deadly.

A wave of nausea distracted him for a moment. He staggered, reached for support. A gentle hand steadied him. Turning his head, he looked into a pair of large bright-green eyes.

"I worried," Reyna whispered, concerned.

He padded her hand. "I am fine." His attention shifted back to Angela.

"The Xandra will tolerate no more violence against her children." Angela spoke with a loud voice. "Let it be known that from this day on those who break her law will be punished. As a sign of good will, she allows you to go home. Spread the news and live in peace with the children of the Xandra. The Mother does not wish to go to war with the True-Humans, but she will, if provoked. Her wrath will be terrible."

"Quite some performance you've arranged there," Massater whispered beside Beringer. "Do you really think you can change the way things work on this planet?"

"You may not believe me, Massater, but I had little to do with this. I am as surprised as you are. Besides, I think this Angel is the real thing. I mean, she's not a real angel, but she speaks for the Xandra. And she isn't bluffing. Look into her eyes, don't you feel the power?"

Massater snorted. "Cheap theatrics. I've seen hypnotists before."

Another figure came out of the shuttle, climbed down the steps. At first Beringer mistook the figure for a man, dressed in a camouflage outfit that seemed a little too large, but then he saw the stranger's face and realized this was a woman, her black hair short-cropped, military style. She had light skin and slightly slanted gray eyes.

"I am Captain Mirtin Koyo," she said, stopping in front of Massater. "I have orders to relieve you of your post, Colonel Massater."

Massater stared at her, then at Beringer. "What is this?" he asked, annoyance showing in his voice and face. "Is this some ploy to get me off this planet? Who are you working for?"

Beringer shrugged. "I've never met this woman before."

Massater took a step toward the woman, looked into her eyes. "You're not even wearing the right uniform."

"I can explain, sir."

"I bet you can."

The woman swallowed, drew herself up and sucked in a deep breath. She let it out with explosive force. "Listen, Colonel Massater. They told me you'd be difficult. Ever since I landed on this damned planet things went wrong. I've been held captive in a dark stinking cave; I've been raped, humiliated, nearly killed, and I am in no mood to exchange pleasantries. I have orders to bring you back, in chains, if necessary. Do I make myself clear, sir?"

Massater's eyes narrowed. "I could have you shot for insubordination, Captain. I am a colonel, don't you forget that."

"You *were* a colonel, Massater. Don't *you* forget that! I've read your file. In detail."

Smiling ruefully, Massater stepped back. His shoulders slumped visibly. He looked suddenly old and tired. "I've been stuck here for a whole year and not much to show for it. Maybe I should thank you for getting me off this hellhole, Captain Koyo. You are welcome to change places with me."

"I have no such intentions, Colonel. This is a rescue-mission. We thought you were lost, possibly dead. You are lucky you have friends in high places who were not willing to let you rot in this *hellhole*, as you put it."

"Thank you, Captain." Massater pointed at the Lander. "What are you doing with such an antique vessel?"

Mirtin allowed herself a tight smile. "I found myself in need of rescue, also, sir. I will explain later, for now, let's get a move on. I don't know how long we can keep the natives at bay."

Massater scanned the compound, looked at he soldiers, who were watching. "They are not natives. They are humans, like you and I, Captain, trying to make sense out of their world. A world they never chose in the first place. I thought I could make a difference, but I was wrong." He shrugged. "Let's go."

Before he could move, one of the soldiers rushed toward him, brandishing a rifle.

Corpo Tivek.

He stopped in front of Massater, his eyes wide with madness under his bushy eyebrows. "I never trusted you, Massater." His voice sounded harsh, almost hysterical. "You might have fooled General Rodriguez, but not me. Now here is proof, you are one of them!"

"Who is *them*, Corpo Tivek?" Massater asked calmly.

"The new breed of Xandra-born, who else?"

Massater chuckled. "You're a fool, Tivek. A poor, ignorant savage you may be, but nevertheless a fool."

"Don't insult me with your superior wisdom, Colonel Massater," Tivek snarled. "All this talk about trying to live in peace with people who are different, now it makes sense. You heard it, the Xandra declared war on us. If we don't defend ourselves, the Great Mother will wipe out all True-Humans." He glared at Beringer. "I never did believe that story about you being a visitor from across the water." His eyes narrowed and his rifle came up.

Before Beringer could react, a bright beam flashed in Colonel Massater's hand and Corpo Tivek stiffened, then he toppled slowly to the ground. Beringer smelled the reek of burned leather and flesh and stared at the small, black hole in the left side of the man's coat.

Someone pulled Beringer down. As he tumbled into the trampled dirt, he heard shots, then screams. He looked to see a group of soldiers advancing toward the shuttle. Some of them stumbled, fell. Beams of light from the shuttle burned them down, until all lay unmoving on the ground.

"Stop the attacks or we will exterminate you all!" a male voice boomed from the shuttle's speakers.

Another tongue of light lashed at the General's tent, it burst into flames.

"Damn it!" cursed Massater. "There go all my reports."

"Forget them," Mirtin said, "let's get into the Lander."

Beringer rose to his feet, with Reyna's help. He found it increasingly difficult to move.

The winged girl spread her wings wide, took to the air. She circled the camp once, and then she disappeared into the clouds.

Starmote watched Beringer come closer. "Are you injured, Commander?" she inquired, her voice loud and clear inside his head.

"No," he said, his voice barely a whisper. "Just get me out of here."

A strong hand gripped his arm, pulled him along. Only vaguely he saw Lt. Wang beside him, felt himself pushed into the shuttle, where he sank gratefully into one of the seats. Someone held his hand, a pair of green eyes stared into his, a gentle female voice spoke soothingly to him, but he felt too tired to listen to the words.

"Take her up!" a man's voice commanded.

The last thing he remembered was the slight vibration of the floor when the shuttle lifted.

Chapter Five

Why the Xandra suggested that he not search out the stranger, who rescued him from certain death, Viran didn't know, but he honored her wish. Now he watched as Angela joined the stranger with Mirtin and Vienne in the flying vessel.

He spent the rest of the night in Angela's embrace, watched her beautiful face contort in the throes of her orgasm as she churned her slim hips above him. She had never known the pleasure of a sexual union before, now she seemed insatiable. Again, he wondered if the Great Mother had indeed done her a service by giving her the means to let a male enter her body, but he recalled the Xandra's words to Angela: *it will pass.*

The oblong disk rose slowly into the air, then it whisked away, disappeared into the cloudy sky.

"A time of changes has come upon our world again," a soft voice said beside him.

He had heard her come, had sensed her presence as she stopped by his side. Turning his head, he looked into her green eyes. "Will it be violent?" he asked.

The Xandra smiled, then she stared at the partially obscured sun. "Changes are always violent, Viran," she murmured and sighed. "I would prefer to walk a different path, but the humans leave me no choice."

"How do I fit into all of this? I am just a simple warrior."

Her hand felt warm on his arm. "You are much more than that," she said gently. When he looked into her beautiful face and listened to her gentle voice, he found it hard to imagine that she was not really human. He knew that the mind, which occupied this soft-spoken female body, was part of a greater intelligence, so alien and powerful that a human mind could never even begin to grasp its potential.

Part of her was inside him, but he was not part of her.

Her green eyes studied his face. "I have chosen you to be my champion, Viran. You are not the first, but you will be the greatest of them all. Your name will be known among the stars. They will write songs about you."

Viran laughed. "I hope I will be alive to hear them. All the songs my people sing around the campfires are songs about dead heroes."

"Your essence will be immortal, I promise you that." She pointed into the sky, at a flock of winged creatures. "Those are my eyes. They can only observe, but you will be my arm." Stroking his biceps, she leaned against him for a moment, then she broke away. When he reached for her, she laughed. "There is no time for that now. I want you to go to the City. I will be there, in a different body, but it will be me."

"I don't know the way. How will I get there?"

Viran turned when he heard the sound of hoofs coming out of the small forest behind them. On the path appeared a large brown-coated animal, he recognized it for what it was…a horse.

A man sat on its broad back, a big man, massive and wide-shouldered. Slightly behind the first animal came another one. It had a shiny black coat. A short rope tethered it to the brown horse.

"Meet Tegron," the Xandra said when the man reined in before them. "He will guide you to the City."

Tegron smiled down at them. "You must be Viran," he said with a pleasant baritone voice.

Viran shot an inquiring look at the Xandra. She just shrugged and said, "It is time to go, now."

Viran, still naked, looked down at himself. "I am not ready," he said with a wry grin. "I have no clothing and no weapon."

Before he saw the three men walking down the path, his acute senses had already told him of their coming. One carried a war-hammer, similar to the one he had lost; the other two were loaded down with clothing and supplies.

Recognizing his old leather-breeches and boots, he took them and stepped into them. Then he took the offered sleeveless shirt and examined it.

"I had it made especially for you from the finest leather available. It is made from the skins of a dozen *Dar-birds,*" the Xandra said, smiling, and watched Viran as he put it on.

"That is not my hammer," Viran said, pointing at the weapon.

"I know. I didn't think you would want it back. After all, it almost killed you." The Xandra took the hammer away from the man who carried it. She hefted it easily, handed it to Viran. "Try it. You will find it to be superbly balanced."

Viran's fingers gripped the handle of the weapon, then he stepped back and swung the war-hammer above his head, whirled it around. "It feels light, but handles well."

"You are correct--it is lighter than your old one."

34

"It will take getting used to it," Viran growled. "The head needs to be heavy to smash the skull of an enemy."

"It'll also slow you down. You will be able to crack more skulls, and just as easily with this one." She took another item from one of the men and held it out to Viran, a knife with a long, shiny blade. There were intricate carvings on the handle. "This is a special gift from John Lambert, the man who rescued you. I traded it from him."

Viran ran his finger carefully along the thin blade. He had seen a knife like this one before. Mirtin, the dark-haired stranger, had carried one similar to it, strapped to her boot.

"I am honored to have a weapon like this," he said. "Thank you."

"This comes with it." The Xandra reached around Viran and strapped a belt around his waist, then she took the knife and slipped it into a sheath attached to the belt.

She stood on tiptoes and kissed him gently on the lips. When her lips touched his, he felt a warm tingle rush through his body. "I will be with you, always," she whispered softly. "Now, go."

He grabbed the satchel she gave him and slung it across his shoulders, then he swung himself onto the back of the black horse. Even though he had never ridden before, somehow he knew what to do.

His new companion, Tegron, grinned at him, slapped his own horse gently on the rump and took off. Viran clamped his legs around the belly of his mount and clucked his tongue. The horse shook its thick shaggy mane and neighed loudly, then it followed Tegron. Viran sensed the wildness and power that needed to be brought under control. Instinctively part of his mind reached out to probe the animal-mind. The contact seemed like touching the flower of a *Stinger-Plant*. Nothing concrete, just a gentle tingling, but he knew the horse felt his prodding. It quivered like a young virgin under her lover's touch.

"Easy, my friend," Viran whispered and stroked the trembling flank. The animal calmed down, slowed to a comfortable trot.

"The Mother was right," Tegron said when Viran reached him.

"Right in what?" Viran inquired and pulled gently on his mount's reins.

"She said that you command the *Power*." He grinned. "I didn't expect you to stay on his back. His name is *Wild Spirit*. I raised him from a small foal. He is the brother of my horse, *Lone Walker*. He accepts you."

Viran studied the other man. Big, well-muscled, he carried himself with an air of superiority. His black hair reached almost to his shoulders. A thin dark mustache adorned his upper lip.

Viran noticed that Tegron didn't wear trousers, but a leather kilt. He had draped a short cape around his broad shoulders. "You are Xandra-born," Viran stated.

Tegron's dark eyes narrowed. "Xandra-born don't have facial hair." He pointed to his mustache.

Viran smiled. "I meant no offence. But you were never born by a woman. Your womb was a seed-pod, this I know." He held out a hand. "I do not think less of you. We are brothers."

Laughing, Tegron clamped his fingers around Viran's forearm. "You truly have the Power. I am your humble servant." Digging his heels into his mount's soft belly, Tegron rode off again, slower this time.

They followed a path that ran parallel to the river, until they came to the foot of the cliffs that surrounded the valley. The river became narrow here and ended at the cliff-wall, where it disappeared inside a break in the craggy rocks.

The men dismounted and led their horses into the narrow gap. Entering the dark tunnel, Viran could hear the sound of falling water. When they reached the end of the tunnel, a wall of water blocked their way.

Without hesitating Tegron walked through it, pulling his horse with him. The animal did not shy away. Obviously, it had come this way before.

Viran padded Wild Spirit's flank. "Come," he said and followed his companion. Drenched, they came out on the other side. A large pond lay before them, protected on all sides by tall trees. Tegron already moved towards the shore on the other side.

Viran looked back at the waterfall. The water seemed to come right out of the rocks, most likely fed by an underground river inside the cliffs.

Beside him, Wild Spirit shook himself, spraying Viran with a small shower. Viran stood up to his waist in the water. It wasn't cold, but he felt uncomfortable with his wet breeches.

"Let's get out of the water onto dry land," he said to the horse. "You may like the water. I don't."

They entered the forest. The path they were on seemed well traveled.

"This is the only path that leads to Sanctuary from this side," Tegron explained. "Only Xandra-born use it to bring trade-goods. You may not see them, but there are sentries everywhere, who will warn the Mother of any unwanted intruders."

Viran didn't see anyone, but he sensed the presence of the Watchers. His hand went to the head of his war-hammer, which he carried in a sling strapped to his back. However, he knew he didn't have to worry about danger for him here.

* * * *

The path lay in semidarkness. Had there been roots and other growth covering the path they would have made slower progress.

Viran had adjusted to the gait of the horse and felt almost comfortable on the small blanket draped across the animal's back.

They traveled all day, stopping only once at midday to eat. Tegron took dried cakes and some fruit out of one of the two bags, which hung in front of him across the back of his horse.

Late in the afternoon, they arrived at the edge of the forest. Ahead of them lay a wide-open grassy valley.

"I'd like to spend the night in the shelter of the trees," Tegron said, squinting into the overcast sky. Light drizzle promised a cold and wet night.

"I agree." Viran said, glad for the garment that covered his upper torso, but wishing for Tegron's cape.

"There is a path not far from here. It leads to a small, secluded pond. Large Ocla-trees grow there. The roots will provide protection, and their fruit is sweet."

Viran nodded. He remembered the last time he'd searched for shelter under gnarled roots. "Are there any Zombs in this place?" he asked.

Tegron twisted his body around to look at Viran. "Not as far as I know. They prefer the caves in the mountains. However, the scavengers are fierce in the valley. They've been known to attack sleepers for lack of rotting corpses."

Before they took the narrow path, back into the forest Tegron climbed from his horse, squatted down and studied the ground. "Riders passed this way not long ago," he commented.

Viran saw the hoof prints in the soft soil without getting off his horse. "Who?" he asked.

Tegron shook his head. "Nobody uses this trail, except *Rendas*."

Viran could see the footprints of small hoofs, but they were old and much smaller than the one's Tegron examined.

Entering the trail, they found it dark and barely wide enough for the horses. They followed it slowly and with caution. Viran listened to the sounds around them. Most of them were familiar.

A loud crack, like the breaking of a dry branch, interrupted the chatter and chirping of the small forest creatures. In the silence that followed Viran heard the laughter of men. He knew what had caused that sound. His hand went to his chest. The memory of that night would be with him for a long time.

Tegron's horse had stopped moving. Tegron slipped off his horse, beckoned. Viran nodded grimly, dismounted silently. Another shot broke the silence. More whooping laughter. Viran put his hand over Wild Spirit's flaring nostril. "Calm down," he whispered, his mind reaching out to calm the animal. The horse relaxed and lowered its head.

Squeezing past Lone Walker, Viran followed his companion who moved slowly and silently down the dark winding trail. Tegron stopped when they came to a sharp bend in the path, put his finger against his lips. They could hear voices and low laughter, then the explosive sound of another shot.

Tegron made a motion for Viran to stay, then he got onto his belly and crawled away. Viran waited for a moment. When Tegron didn't come back, he removed his war-hammer from its loop and stepped around the bend into a small open glade. He saw five horses tethered to trees, just as many men standing up to their waist in the still water of the pond, and he saw Tegron swinging something over his head.

One of the men was aiming his rifle at a form rising out of the water. Viran swallowed hard, suppressing a cry of anguish and outrage.

The frail white body of a winged girl stood in the opened shell of a seedpod. Her silvery wings unfolded slowly behind her as she stared with large blue eyes at the man in front of her. She had a smile on her lovely face.

Fire sprouted out of the long barrel of the rifle, the thunder of the sudden explosion painful in Viran's ears. His fingers grabbed the handle of his war-hammer in a crushing grip and he watched in horror as the angel fell backwards. Her wings were still spread, and she floated toward the water surface in slow motion.

Then she lay unmoving on her back, a river of red stained her white body. Viran counted three more dead angels floating on the water. Before he could react to the violence, he had just witnessed the man who had murdered the angel staggered and collapsed.

On the shore, Tegron stood wide legged. From his right hand hung a small pouch he had tied to a pair of leather thongs. He reached into one of his pockets, removed an object, it looked like a round stone, and put it into the small pouch. Then he began whirling it again over his head.

The four other men in the water spotted him and one of them shouted, lifted his rifle. Viran sprang forward, uttering a piercing war cry. The man with the rifle hesitated, momentarily distracted by Viran's sudden appearance. Tegron released the stone; it smashed into the rifleman's head, silencing him.

In the middle of the pond floated the tattered remains of a Xandra-plant. Viran also saw a few closed seedpods on the other side, close to shore. One of them split open, while Viran watched. An angel sat up and looked around.

Viran stood at the edge of the pond and swung his war-hammer in a threatening gesture as one of the three remaining men turned toward the rising angel. "Don't touch her or I'll crack your skull wide open!" Viran bellowed.

The man looked at Viran. "She's a creature of the Xandra. She must be destroyed!" he shouted.

"She has a right to live, but you don't!" Tegron let another rock fly, but the missile didn't reach its target.

Viran didn't see any rifles in the hands of the three men, just long, wooden clubs. All of the men were bare-chested. On the shore, beside the horses, Viran saw heaps of clothing and a few rifles.

These men were no threat to him.

"Come out of the water and leave this place," Viran spoke quietly, but loud enough for them to hear. "We will spare your lives, enough blood has been spilled."

The men whispered to each other, then they came wading toward shore. Before they reached dry land, Viran walked over to where their clothing lay and picked up a couple of rifles. He didn't know how they worked, but he was not ignorant about their deadliness. Tegron joined him, picked up another one and threw it into the water.

The men in the pond protested loudly, but Tegron ignored them.

"They won't murder another living being with these," he said to Viran. "The water will make them useless."

Viran followed his example and carried the rest of the weapons to the water's edge.

"You've sentenced us to die by taking our rifles," one of the men complained as he climbed onto shore. He was big, muscular. Clenching his fists, he glowered at Viran, and then at Tegron. "Why are you protecting these abominations?" he demanded to know.

"Because I am one of them," Tegron rumbled.

The man's eyes widened in surprise. "But you have facial hair," he said.

"So I have, that doesn't make me human." Tegron glanced at Viran. "No offence to you, my brother."

Viran grinned, but said nothing. He was watching the other two men who were joining their companion on dry land. One of them tall and thin, the other one short and stocky. The stocky one stared angrily at Viran, gripping the club he carried with a white-knuckled hand. "We are three, you are two," he said.

"Yours will be the first head I'll smash, that will leave two of you," Viran growled. He was getting impatient with these men. They were all murderers. The evidence floated on the still water of the pond.

"He's a barbarian," the tall one said to his companions. "Don't goad him." He looked at Viran. "Can we take our horses? All of them?" he asked.

"Take the horses and the rest of your things. Go now, before I lose my patience!"

"I'll get Lone Walker and Wild Spirit," Tegron said. "They are blocking the trail."

Viran nodded.

The three men went to their piles of clothing, slipped into their shirts and donned long, gray coats.

"You are soldiers," Viran observed.

"We *were* soldiers," the big man corrected him. "Our army has been disbanded by a self-proclaimed goddess who came in a flying disc from the sky. Most of our comrades slunk away with their tail tucked between their legs." He pushed out his chest. "I still say it was the Xandra who is playing with our minds. I am not afraid. The Holy War is not over."

"Keep your mouth shut, Marron!" said the stocky one.

"I say what I want."

"I wish your brain was big enough to fill that big skull of yours."

Tegron came back with the horses. The three soldiers swung onto their mounts and left, taking the horses of their dead companions with them.

Viran watched them disappear down the trail. He shook his head when he heard them still arguing as they rode away.

"We should have killed them," he said to Tegron

Tegron gave a short, barking laugh. "The scavengers will take care of that for us, Viran. They won't survive the night."

Chapter Six

"It is the only way."

The female voice and the touch of a soft hand shaking him brought Beringer back to awareness. Opening his eyes, he saw Reyna's concerned face above him. She smiled gently.

"What is going on?" His voice sounded like a croak in his own ears.

"The poison of the Shadow-Angel is in your blood," Reyna said. "There is only one way to make it powerless."

Beringer looked at Starmote who stood behind the Xandra-girl. Starmote shook her head. Her black eyes seemed darker than usual. "There is a foreign substance in your blood that I cannot identify. The night-creature injected it into you, in addition to taking more blood than she should have." She spoke with a grave voice. "I cannot deceive you, Commander. You may be dying."

"No!" protested Reyna vehemently. "He need not die. I can help him."

"She wants to have sex with you," Starmote said and shrugged. "Under the stars, tonight."

"Not under the stars. When Rah and Roh are high our bodies must join."

"Superstitious nonsense." Starmote made a gurgling sound.

"Not superstition. Truth." Reyna touched her breast. "The medicine is within me. It is the Xandra-way."

Looking past Reyna and Starmote, Beringer saw a blond young woman standing in the doorway that led to the pilot's cabin.

"Who are you?" he asked. "By any chance another female who wants to have sex with me?"

The blond woman scowled for a moment, then she smiled. "I am Vienne. You must be the famous Commander Beringer."

Beringer grinned weakly. "Famous, I like that." He closed his eyes to fight off another wave of nausea. When he opened them again, Vienne had come closer. He noticed her bright blue eyes. "Sorry about that remark. Must be the drugs," he said.

She shrugged. "It's alright."

Even though she was dressed in a camouflage outfit too large for her, he found her attractive and quite beautiful. "Are you human?" he asked.

42

She nodded, flashed him another smile. "Not so long ago I would have been offended by that question, but now…" she lifted her slim shoulders again, "…now I am not surprised."

"Beringer." Reyna bent over him. "Let me help you."

He sat up, aware of his pounding heart. The movement made him dizzy. "Where is Lt. Wang?" he asked.

"He stayed behind to help Esram and his family. Also, to make sure that the soldiers don't cause any problems." Starmote spoke without emotion, but her black alien eyes glistened strangely. "You should rest, Commander."

She had removed the hood that covered her head. The cape, which she wrapped around herself, stood partially open to reveal her naked breasts. He could see the faint markings that crisscrossed her fair skin.

She saw him look, drew the cape closer around her body. "We'll meet Wang and the others when they reach the city's outskirts. Then we will join them again. We don't want to attract too much attention to the shuttle." She paused. "I assumed temporary command while you were incapacitated."

"That's alright." Beringer got to his feet, swayed, aware of a buzzing in his ears that had not been there before. He walked through the door into the front cabin. Lambert sat in the pilot's chair, watching the screens. He turned his head to look at Beringer. "Commander," he said, "You're up."

I must be sick, Beringer thought, *even Lambert can't hide it*. He grinned sourly. "I'm up, for how long, I don't know. Starmote tells me I'm dying."

"I said *you may be dying*," Starmote said from behind him. "I'll find an antidote, just give me some time."

Scanning the cabin, Beringer saw Colonel Massater and the dark-haired woman. He didn't remember her name. She gave him a curt nod when he looked at her. "I am Lt. Royo," she said. "Maybe I can help. I've had medical training." She smiled ruefully. "Unfortunately, I had to leave my equipment behind. Vienne and I were lucky to get away with our lives."

"You were the reason why Lambert had to leave his post?" Beringer asked.

"I'm afraid not. There was someone else. We just came along for the ride, but we are grateful anyway."

Beringer sank into the co-pilot's chair, swiveled it around so he could look at the woman and Massater. The Colonel sat on one of the couches, which were bolted to the wall. "Colonel Massater, you don't look very happy."

The Colonel gave Beringer a long look. "Skip the Colonel, Beringer, just call me Massater. As of now I am retired."

"Don't be so pessimistic, Colonel," the woman beside him said. "Maybe you'll be reinstated. After all, you *did* spend a whole year on this planet. There must be some useful information you have gathered."

Massater chuckled. "I'll be lucky if I don't end up in front of a firing squad. Let's face it--I lost my team, my equipment. All my recordings went up in flames. I have stood by as untold beings were slaughtered by the people I associated with. You're right, they'll probably give me a medal."

Beringer had listened quietly to the other man's tirade. Looking at the dark-haired woman, he said, "Captain Royo, I don't know how much Lambert has told you about us and how much information you have given him. I haven't spoken to him yet, and now is not the time. Since you are in my shuttle I think it would be a good idea if I knew more about you, your background and your mission on this planet."

The woman nodded. "As I told you before, my name is Mirtin Koyo. I am a captain with the *Alliance Space Force*. Special Services. I was sent here to find Colonel Massater and bring him back."

The Commander lifted his hand to wipe the perspiration from his forehead. He felt suddenly warm and chilly at the same time. His hand trembled slightly when he looked at the moisture on his fingers. The buzzing in his ears seemed do drown out the humming of the shuttle's engine. He just wanted to lie down and sink into oblivion. Just to speak proved to be an effort. "Why do I have the feeling you're not telling me everything, Captain?"

"I don't know who you really are, Commander Beringer. As far as I know you might be a spy for the *Solar Union.*"

Despite the rotten way Beringer felt, he laughed out loud.

"What's the joke?" Mirtin asked.

It was Massater who answered. "The Commander has never even heard of the Solar Union, or the Alliance. He made a sweeping gesture toward Beringer. "Captain Koyo, may I introduce to you Commander Les Beringer of the Terran Space Navy?"

"If you are having fun at my expense, I am not amused. By *Terra* you mean Earth, I assume, unless you are talking about a colony nobody knows about."

"No colony. It's good old Earth all right. A thousand years ago." Massater chuckled. "I'm surprised, Captain. This ancient relic we are riding in should have given you some clues. Look at the insignia on the borrowed uniform you are wearing."

Mirtin's gray eyes widened. "You are from the past?" she asked Beringer.

Beringer nodded in agreement. "I was here already a thousand years ago."

The woman shook her head, disbelieving. "You're not telling me that you are an immortal?"

"No."

"Time travel, then?"

"No." Beringer chuckled, amused by the young woman's obvious impatience. "Deep freeze."

"Impossible! We don't have the technology now, and we certainly didn't have it then."

Before Beringer could answer, an urgent voice spoke inside his head. *Careful, Commander*! It almost felt like a stab of pain. He glanced at Starmote, startled. She was watching him. Her alien eyes seemed to draw him toward her. For a fleeting moment, the expression on her face seemed almost feral.

He brushed the perspiration from his brows, tried to steady his shaking hands.

"*Sorry*," her voice came again, gentler this time. "*These may be your people, but they are not your allies--we are. It may be best in our mutual interest not to tell them too much.*"

Beringer looked at Mirtin. "We found some friends." He indicated Starmote. "Without her people's help we would not be here today, but that is of no importance right now. I'd like you to give me a history lesson. Tell me about Earth and the Colonies."

Mirtin sighed, shrugged. "Where do I begin? I am not a historian. Thousand years is a long time."

"I don't want details. I need to know about the political climate. Who are the super-powers?"

"Not Earth, if that's what you are hinting at." Mirtin smiled. "Earth is overpopulated, depleted of most of her resources, hungry for living space. There are the planets of Sol and the large moons of Jupiter, Saturn, and Uranus, also overpopulated. Humans are vigorous breeders, you know."

"What about other systems?"

"Humanity has spread across a large sector of the Galaxy. Over one hundred planets have been discovered and colonized. There was a war five hundred years ago, the *War of Independence*. It lasted almost fifty years. When it was over, Earth had been defeated and the *Alliance of Independent Planets* was founded. Fifty-nine planets belong to the Alliance today. My planet is one of them."

"And the other planets"

"The *Mandarin Empire* owns twenty seven. The rest are either too far away, or not important enough to matter."

"So what is the big deal with this one?"

Mirtin threw a long look at Starmote who had been listening intently. "In two thousand years of space exploration humans have not encountered one star-faring race. None of the discovered planets had intelligent life on it that equaled ours. Along comes this planet. At first, it was thought to be just another lost colony, hostile to any contact. The lack of advanced technology was contributed to the fact that there have always been groups who rejected any advances in knowledge, or rejected technology altogether.

"When none of the contact teams that were sent returned, suspicion was naturally aroused and danger flags went up. This planet was put under quarantine. No unauthorized landings, no contact with the local population until more information had been gathered. Colonel Massater headed one of the exploration teams. When he didn't report back for almost a year, certain people thought him important enough to send a rescue team."

"All that expense and effort to rescue one man? Come on, Captain!"

Mirtin leaned back into her seat. "Some of our agents managed to send reports. They spoke of alien life forms that appeared human, but were not. They talked about magical creatures, of beautiful women with strange powers. Most of it sounded like nonsense, nothing could be backed up scientifically. Then there was that huge derelict spacecraft. It was sealed off, with no way to enter it. We knew it was old, and, we assumed, dead." She looked straight at Starmote. "I guess we were wrong."

Before Starmote could comment, Lambert spoke up. "We'll be landing in a few minutes. Please, secure your stabilizer fields."

Starmote, who had been standing, slipped into the seat beside Beringer. She gave him a quick smile.

"You should get out of that ridiculous outfit," he told her.

A gentle shudder went through the craft as it settled to the ground. "Scanners show no signs of any large life forms in the vicinity," Lambert reported.

"I need some fresh air," Beringer said.

"I'll come with you." Starmote looked concerned.

"No." Beringer waved her back, moved toward the opening entrance door. "I need some time by myself."

The cool evening air felt good on his moist skin. He took a deep breath, detected the now familiar scent of the intoxicating purple flowers. Climbing down the few steps of the short ramp, he stepped onto the soft grass. They had landed in a small clearing. When he spotted the path, he headed for it, entered the semi-darkness of the forest. He didn't walk far, the path ended by a pond. Only a few small plants floated on its still surface. The water splashed gently as a furry creature, the size of a small dog, slid into it.

Beringer sat cross-legged in the grass, stared at the glassy surface of the water. He found it difficult to think straight. His thoughts seemed to wander. He needed rest; maybe he should relinquish command to Starmote.

Her voice startled him. "Are you alright, Commander?"

Looking around, he realized she wasn't here, just her voice inside his head. "I'm fine," he answered, "just a little tired. Don't worry."

He took off his shirt and stretched out on the soft ground. The grass felt cool on his naked skin. He closed his eyes and drifted off into a deep sleep.

When he awoke, it was dark. Above him, the two moons had risen into the now cloudless sky. Then he realized that he wasn't alone. "Reyna," he said to the girl kneeling beside him. "How long have you been here?"

She smiled, put her hand on his naked chest. "Most of the time. I followed you when you left the flying hut." She began to run her hands gently across his chest. He closed his eyes again, enjoying the warm touch of her soft hands. Then he felt her fingers on his belt, heard the snap as they released the buckle. Her hand moved down his belly and touched his manhood.

Even though he didn't remember dreaming, he must have had an erotic dream, or it could have been the strong fragrance of the flowers that grew along the shore of the pond that caused his erection. His penis became hard inside Reyna's hand; he groaned, didn't object when she tugged on his pants.

His eyes opened to watch her straddle him. She stood still for a moment, pulled the gray robe over her head and discarded it. His gaze fastened on her full breasts, traveled down her smooth belly to her hairless puffy mound. One of her hands went to his rigid penis and guided it toward her womanhood.

When her hot wet sheath closed over his aching member, he groaned loudly and reached for her slim hips. He pulled her down, lunged upwards and entered her deeply. Her inner muscles tightened around him and began to vibrate gently.

"Relax, Beringer," she whispered. "I give to you myself--and I will give you great pleasure."

When he searched her face, she smiled down at him. Her green eyes bored into his. Her tongue darted like a pink snake across her red lips. She gyrated above him, slowly, ever so slowly. Then she bent forward, offered her breast. "Drink the nectar from my body," she whispered. "It will give you strength, make you well."

He took the long nipple into his mouth, began to suck. Eagerly, he swallowed the sweet liquid that flowed from her breast. Strength surged through his body as he drank the elixir. His arms went around her slim body and turned with her to be on top. Her knees bent as she pulled her legs up, her thighs opened wide to give him greater freedom to move. With forceful thrusts, he entered her again and again. She gasped, drew his lips toward hers. When he kissed her, she snaked her tongue into his mouth. He sucked on it and swallowed the liquid from her tongue.

His orgasm came with tremendous force. He slammed his body into hers. She cried out when the torrent broke lose from his penis to flood her soft, greedily sucking orifice.

Pulling out of her, he found himself still hard. She sat up, turned onto her knees and pushed up her round buttocks. Between them, her pink sex-organ beckoned him to enter her again. He cupped her slender body. She reached up between her slightly spread legs and grabbed his penis, pulled it forward. Easily he slipped back into her. His hips snapped back and forth with a steady rhythm. Breathing deeply, he became aware again of the pungent fragrance in the air.

Above him, the two moons shone brightly. They had moved higher in the sky. Soon they would almost touch and then move apart again. His mind suddenly clear, he looked down at the naked slim body of the girl who knelt in front of him. Her round buttocks clenched together every time he pushed forward. Inside her tight softness, his penis felt large and as hard as a rock.

His hands went around her chest to cup her solid breasts. She turned her head, looked back at him with green eyes that were partially obscured by her cascading red hair. He saw her smile, heard her soft laughter. Then she began to move her hips, milking his swollen penis with great enthusiasm.

Coming inside her again, he suppressed the roar that rumbled deep in his throat. Never before had he experienced a climax as intense and long as this one. When it finally ended, he relaxed his body. Reyna sank to the ground. He rested on top of her, breathing hard, his erect member still buried inside her.

After awhile she wriggled underneath him. "You are heavy," she said.

He pushed himself up on his elbows, pulled out and rolled over onto his back. Reyna sat up, giggled happily when she saw his erect organ. "I am glad to see you feel better," she said. She rose to her feet and held out a hand to pull him up.

Out of the trees behind her stepped a tall dark figure, trailing what seemed like a cloak. Then the cloak opened and became a pair of wings.

"I've watched you," a familiar female voice said softly.

Reyna gasped in surprise, stepped backward, her hands held in front of her.

"Naomi," Beringer said hoarsely. "How did you find me?"

"You and I are linked," the Shadow Angel said. "You need me as much as I need you."

"Last time you nearly killed me." Beringer got himself into a sitting position and stared up the winged girl silhouetted against the two moons.

"I lost control, and so did you," she said. "I took too much and gave too much."

"You poisoned him with the vile liquid that flows inside you," Reyna said with an accusing voice.

The Shadow-Angel's dark eyes fastened on the Xandra-girl. "Leave us!" she commanded.

Reyna shrieked and ran away.

Naomi laughed, then she stepped closer to Beringer, loomed over him and pushed him onto his back with one strong hand. Standing wide legged above him, she lowered herself into his lap. The touch of her sex-organ felt like a searing flame, and then his rigid pole slid into a hot inferno.

Beringer was still in a high state of arousal from the fragrance of the purple flowers, now stronger than ever, and from the intoxicating substance from Reyna's breasts. He called out with a hoarse voice and lifted his hips off the ground to meet Naomi's thrust. Her hips began to snap forward with increasing speed and the pleasure he experienced proved nearly unbearable. She stretched out on top of him, pushing her nipple into his mouth. She tasted different from Reyna, but the liquid he swallowed was sweet and addictive.

"Now!" she hissed, her vagina milking him with savage force.

He exploded inside her, only barely aware of the sting in his neck when she sank her needle-fangs into his artery. At first, he experienced only pleasure. After awhile he began to feel drowsy and his strength ebbed out of him.

Deep inside him something screamed a warning. When he tried to push her off, he found her too strong. Her legs and arms pinned him to the ground, her mouth sucked steadily and greedily.

Suddenly, she ripped her fangs out of his neck and screamed. With a violent motion, she rolled away from him.

Someone bent over him. "I'm sorry, Beringer, I could not help you. But I called your friends." Reyna stroked his cheek with gentle fingers. He tried to raise himself up, but felt too weak, his arms and legs like lead. Turning his head, he saw Starmote standing over the unmoving form of the Shadow-Angel. Beside her stood John Lambert, a gun in his hand.

"Is she dead?" Lambert asked.

Starmote bent down, held something against Naomi's neck. Straightening up, she said, "She's dead. I had no choice."

She came to kneel beside Beringer. "Are you alright, Commander?"

Beringer shook his head with great effort. "I can't move. I seem to be paralyzed."

Starmote ran her scanning device along Beringer's body, scowled. Then she looked at Reyna.

The Xandra-girl sobbed. "He was fine before the Shadow-Angel came."

"Well, he is not fine now. I can't help him."

"The Great Mother can heal him. We must take him to the City."

Starmote looked down at Beringer. "I'm sorry, Commander," she said. "The creature drained much of your blood, which is why you are weak. The paralysis is caused by an unknown substance. I don't know what to do."

"Take me to the City," Beringer whispered. He was slipping in and out of consciousness. "Take me to the Xandra."

Blackness engulfed him like a dark cloak, shutting off his senses.

Chapter Seven

His limp hand felt cold and lifeless, but he was not dead, just unconscious.

"Beringer," she whispered. "The Mother will help you." She looked at the woman who looked like a Water-Nymph, but wasn't. "We must hurry, there is little time," she said.

The large nymph-eyes glistened darkly. She called herself Starmote. Reyna sensed the mental and physical powers this woman possessed. She was not from this world.

"We'll get him there as fast as we can." Starmote said. "Until then there is nothing you can do. Why don't you get some rest?"

Reyna held on to Beringer's hand. "I'll stay right here with him," she said stubbornly. She watched Starmote settle into her seat and close her eyes. Beside Starmote sat one of the alien women. She was thin and had hair as bright as the fur of a *Mountain-Skat* in winter. Vienne, they called her. In the seat, opposite of her sat her companion, the other True-Human female. Mirtin. The gaunt man beside her was Massater.

True-Humans believed that Xandra-born were stupid and incapable of thinking clear thoughts, but Reyna knew that they were wrong. She had an excellent memory for names and places. And she could learn. Most Xandra-born did not have the desire to learn. After all, they were born with certain knowledge. Xandra-born were not ambitious, not like the True-Humans, who seemed driven by greed and lust, and much hatred, mostly toward the creatures of the Great Mother.

Reyna didn't know why. Born with a great capacity for love, she did not understand the concept of hate. Her eyes rested on Beringer's slack face. Smiling, she stroked his cheek. Beringer was different from the True-Humans of her world. Strong in mind and body, he had shown no hate or distaste for the children of the Xandra.

She knew she loved him.

But now he may be dying.

She leaned her head against his hand and closed her eyes. When she opened them again, she felt the floor under her feet vibrating gently. It seemed to fall away from her. She experienced a strange sensation in her belly.

"I found a place where we can land. There is a large, walled-in structure nearby. The image shows a few ponds. I detect many life signs inside the buildings." She recognized the voice of John Lambert, the True-Human, who controlled the flying hut. They called it a *Shuttle*. She must use the correct name.

"That is the Temple of the Mother," Reyna said.

The feeling of falling stopped. Reyna looked at the rectangular hole that suddenly appeared in one of the walls. She looked out at the night sky and inhaled the cool, humid air that entered the cabin.

"We'll have to put him on the floater," Lambert said.

Reyna moved reluctantly out of the way when Starmote gave her a gentle shove. Lambert removed a long, flat board from a niche in the wall, laid it on the floor. The he and Starmote put Beringer on it. Lambert did something and the floater lifted into the air.

"You stay with the shuttle," Starmote said to Lambert. "Reyna and I will take the Commander to the Xandra." She looked at Reyna and said, "I hope you know where we are going."

Reyna nodded her head. "I know. I've been here before."

They stepped onto soft grass. There were trees around them, tall trees with wide-spreading branches, laden with yellow berries. Reyna remembered this place, an orchard near the Temple.

"This way," she said and began walking. Underneath her naked feet, the grass felt wet and the smell of a recent rainfall clung to the soil that covered the roots of the trees.

Starmote walked beside her, pulling the floater that carried the unconscious body of Beringer with apparent ease. Reyna didn't waste any time thinking about all the wonders she had seen since meeting Beringer and his companions. This floater happened to be just another of them.

In the pale light of the two moons Rah and Roh, they found a trail that led toward the high walls, which surrounded the Temple of the Mother. It ended in front of a small wooden door set into the massive stones. Reyna pounded against the door and moments later, it opened. A hooded figure stepped through the opening, one of the temple guards.

"Why are you not using the designated gates?" The voice sounded harsh, and gravelly.

"Forgive me, but we must see the Great Mother immediately," Reyna stammered. "A man is dying." She indicated the still figure of Beringer.

"Many who come here are dying." The guard sounded cold and bored. "What makes this one so special?"

"His name is Beringer. He lay with a Shadow-Angel."

"He is not the first."

"He is a messenger from the stars."

The hooded figure stepped closer, stared at Starmote. "You are not Xandra, nor are you human," he stated.

"You are correct. I am neither," Starmote said coolly.

Reyna touched the guard's cloak. "She is a *Sky-Goddess.*"

The guard stayed silent for a moment, and then he stepped back into the dark entranceway. "You may enter. Leave your clothing behind!"

"Why?" Starmote asked, defiantly.

"Because you are not allowed to take any weapons into the temple. You carry weapons."

"For my protection. I do not know what dangers I will be facing."

"No harm will come to you inside the Temple of the Xandra. When you leave, your possessions will be returned to you. Now, get undressed!" The guard barred the way, his tone cold, almost menacing.

Starmote removed her clothing, standing naked in the cool air. Reyna pulled her simple dress over her head and handed it to the hooded figure. She became aware of another presence. Another hooded figure, huge and bulky. "I will carry the man," a thick, guttural voice came from inside the hood.

Starmote didn't protest when the big guard lifted Beringer from the floater. Beringer was not a small man, but the guard picked him up as if he weighed nothing.

Out of an alcove in the wall stepped a small female, a *Sprite*, carrying a glow-stone. From her shoulders sprouted a pair of transparent wings. They were too small to be of any use. Sprites could not fly.

"Follow me," the Sprite said with the high soft voice typical for her kind. She turned and walked back into the alcove. Reyna discovered that it was actually a doorway that led into a small chamber. When she saw the gaping hole in the ground, she knew that they would be taken below ground to the heart of the Great Mother.

Soon they were climbing down a set of stairs hewn into the rocks. Down and down they descended into an underground cavern. From above hung shiny stalactites, long and thin, like giant icicles, covered with small glow stones. Multicolored crystals that grew on the walls, the floor, and the roof of the cavern reflected their light.

Deeper and deeper they climbed. Sometimes there were stairs, and sometimes they walked on a sloping, slippery surface. The air felt damp and hot on Reyna's naked skin and droplets of perspiration soon covered her body.

The little Sprite danced ahead of them on light feet. The giant guard walked behind her, carrying the prone body of Beringer. Starmote stayed close to the hooded figure, as if she worried that he might run away with her commander.

Reyna smiled to herself. She knew that there was no danger here.

The floor they walked on leveled out, the cavern widened, became huge. In front of them lay a giant lake, its placid surface almost totally covered with a carpet of purple flowers.

Reyna's heart began to beat faster, the breath caught in her throat, excitement rushed through her like a roaring wind. She stood in the presence of the Great Mother. This was the heart of the Xandra. Only a few chosen were ever allowed to enter here.

A couple of giant hounds barred their way. Bare teeth gleamed in huge mouths, saliva dripped onto the ground as the hounds loomed over their visitors. The red eyes glowed with intelligence and Reyna cowered back as one of them lowered its large head to stare at her.

The little Sprite spoke a few words, then touched the hound's shaggy flank. "They look meaner than they are," she said to Reyna and Starmote. Laughing, she slapped the other hound on the rump. The hound growled and moved aside.

Reyna glanced at the mountain of white bones that filled a hollow in the ground nearby, not quite convinced by the Sprite's words.

The giant, who carried Beringer, moved forward and headed for the lake. When Reyna and Starmote tried to follow, the Sprite held them back. "He will be taken care of, don't worry," she assured them and began walking toward another set of steps. They led upward in a tight spiral. "Come," she said.

The staircase proved steep and the steps slippery. Reyna held on to the thick rope knotted around stone pillars, which were set into the steps at regular intervals, forming a somewhat safe railing.

Breathing became difficult in the humid air, and Reyna let out a sigh of relief when they finally reached the top of the stairs. They emerged inside a small room. A series of glow-rocks set into the ceiling illuminated the brightly painted walls and floor. A door led them into a garden filled with people. In the pale light of the two Wanderers Reyna could see that most of them were engaged, collecting seeds for the Xandra.

A water-nymph appeared in front of them, carrying two cups. She handed one to Reyna and the other one to Starmote. "Welcome to the *Celebration of Harvest,*" the nymph said. "Drink from the *Holy Elixir of the Mother.*"

Reyna accepted the cup, drank deeply. The power of the Xandra entered her veins, filled her with joy and longing. She ran to a pond close by and dove into the water. Groping around, she found what she needed, and with gentle fingers she laid the thin transparent seed-pouch onto her genitals, watched it mold itself to her body.

When she climbed onto shore, she caught the eye of a human male. He was young, handsome. She smiled at him and watched him walk toward her, his seed-giver hard and solid, and she could hardly wait to feel him inside her.

He took her into his arms and kissed her. She pulled him down on top of her. Spreading her legs wide, she waited for him to enter her. He stabbed frantically, clearly inexperienced. Reyna took hold of his pole, guided him, and pushed up against him when she felt him slide into her eager vessel.

A shock ran through her body, pleasure spread from her genitals into her belly, breasts, limbs. She offered him her breast. His lips closed over her nipple and he began to suck greedily. It wasn't long before he shook in her embrace. She milked his gushing spout, letting him fill the seed-pouch inside her belly with his precious seed. Ecstasy flooded through her, and she collected every drop. The Mother would be happy with her. She was a good seed-collector.

The young man lay in her arms, breathing heavily. "This is my first time," he said. "Did I do well?"

Reyna held him tight, and then she kissed him gently. "You did well. The Mother will be pleased."

He felt still stiff inside her, and when he began to move again, she pressed her hands against his chest. "I must get another seed-pouch first," she said. Reluctantly, he pulled out of her.

She got up, walked to the pond and stepped into the water. The fertilized pouch slid out of her. She found another one that was ready to receive and let it flow into her seed-channel. Then she ran back to the waiting young human male. This time she knelt in front him on all fours. He got behind her, slid his stiff pole between her slightly spread legs. Pushing up her buttocks, she opened herself to him, felt him slide back into her ready channel.

His hands grabbed her hips, and with steady movements, he began to drive his rigid pole in and out of her.

Reyna closed her eyes and let her awareness be in her belly. Only joy and pleasure existed, nothing else. This was the reason she had been born, to collect seeds for the Mother. The fertilized seed-pouch would grow into a pod and soon another life would enter the world to, hopefully, start the cycle again. What kind of life form would grow inside the pod Reyna did not know. It didn't matter. Only the Xandra knew.

Fire spread through her body when the seed-giver inside her grew and finally exploded with great force.

The young human might be inexperienced, but he proved very capable, his seed-giver still hard, ready to fill another pouch. After letting him drink from her breast, Reyna obtained a fresh seed-pouch. The young male lay on his back when she returned, his eyes closed. Reyna straddled him and impaled herself on his rigid organ. Snapping her hips back and forth, she let her inner muscles ripple across his hard pole. Reyna knew how to give and take pleasure. She'd done this many times.

Xandra-born men were useless as seed-givers, that was the reason Reyna and her sisters had to collect seeds from True-Human males. It was the way. However, she didn't know of any reason why she could not couple with a Xandra-born male. In many ways, Xandra-born had more endurance and stamina than the True-Humans. The pleasure felt the same, possibly even more intense.

The sons of the Xandra were sought after by human women, and not just because coupling with them didn't create any offspring.

Reyna loved joining with a male, any male, Xandra-born or human.

She slowed the movements of her hips and began to rotate her pelvis. Her sheath gripped the stiff pole inside her tightly. The young man underneath her dug his fingers into her breasts, from his lips escaped a loud moan.

"I never knew this could be so beautiful," he said hoarsely, stiffened and cried out as his seed-giver squirted its load with great force into her. Reyna laughed joyfully, collected every drop of his precious gift. He began to shrink inside her. She lifted up, released his now wrinkled, shriveling seed-spout.

The young man looked up at her and grinned hugely. "I think I've dried up," he said, while trying to catch his breath. "Everything I was told is true. This is truly a wonderful experience. I wonder if coupling with a human girl is this good."

Reyna shrugged. "Why not find out?" she asked and looked at one of the couples nearby. Both were True-Humans, a young girl and an older man.

Reyna thought fleetingly of her own age. Even though she didn't appear to be any older than the human girl, she was not young in years. Her *Time of Change* was close.

Humans changed as they grew older, Xandra-born didn't. They stayed young looking, but in the end, they turned into ugly and evil smelling creatures. The humans called them *Zombs*.

She pointed to the other couple. "She's human, why not ask her? I'll gladly collect the man's seeds."

Still grinning, the young man looked at his limp pole.

Reyna smiled. "Let me get a fresh seed-pouch, and then I'll see what I can do."

She returned and knelt beside him. "Come, drink from my breast," she told him. He sat up, crouched in front of her. While he drank, she fondled his seed-giver. Soon he became hard again. Reyna laughed and kissed him. Then she got up and walked over to the other couple.

The older man was behind the young girl, his stiff pole sliding in and out of her belly. Reyna bent over the man, kissed him on the lips. When his lips parted she pushed her tongue into his mouth, let her saliva trickle into it. He moaned and let her push him backwards. When he lay on his back, she hovered over him for a short moment. His mouth moved to her breast, began to suck greedily. She sank into his lap, took his stiff seed-giver deep into her.

When she looked at the abandoned girl beside them, she saw her lying on her back, legs pulled up and wide. The young man knelt between them. He held his stiff mast in one hand, with the other he spread the girl's pink slit. Then he moved forward, stretched out on top of the girl and pushed his seed-giver deep into her seed-catcher.

The girl cried out and wrapped her legs around the young man's torso.

Reyna smiled. Human girls were so emotional, and they didn't have much control. She stared into the man's eyes as she gyrated on top of him. He stared back, but his eyes seemed unfocused. A moan left his mouth, he lunged upward, released his seeds.

He may be old, but his gift is strong, Reyna thought, as she let him fill her vessel.

And it seemed that he was far from being finished. Above her, the two Wanderers were drifting apart, but she had enough time left to collect many more seeds.

Praise the Xandra.

Chapter Eight

The face of the man above her stayed hidden in shadows. In her cradling arms, his back felt broad, the muscles hard, just like his penis that moved in and out of her with a steady rhythm. He filled her almost completely, and she moved against him to take more of him into her.

"You don't have to go on this mission," he said in a familiar voice and slammed his hips into hers. "It is your choice, Mirtin."

"Father?" she gasped and struggled to free herself, but he laughed hollowly, pushed deep into her. "Your choice…" he said, and slam…slam…"Your choice…" slam…slam… His face still hidden in the shadows, his voice repeated over and over, "Your choice… your choice…" as he fucked her with brutal force.

When a sudden ray of light illuminated his face, she screamed and stared in horror at the creature above her. Once the face had been human, not anymore. Now there was only a skull, covered with rotten, decaying scraps of flesh. Yellow stumps of teeth grinned at her from a gaping mouth.

Inside her belly, his penis moved like a living thing. A powerful orgasm racked her body.

"No…" she screamed, "…not like this!"

Suddenly she felt herself falling through empty space. Nothing existed but her screams.

When she opened her eyes, she felt hot and clammy. Disoriented for a moment, she realized she had been dreaming. Her eyes focused on Vienne, who sat across from her, eyes closed. Out of habit, she looked at her wrist, cursed silently when she remembered.

She lost everything she ever owned, including her timepiece. Even the clothes she wore were not her own.

There were no windows in the shuttle, but when she glanced at the screen in the front, she saw darkness. It was still night outside

The alien woman Starmote and the native girl Reyna had left with the dying commander to seek the help of the Xandra, the mythical goddess of this planet. Soon after that, Starmote told Lambert to move the shuttle. How she communicated with him, Mirtin didn't know. Her mind reeled when she thought of everything that happened within these last few days.

Touching the release button of the restraining belt, she stood up to stretch her legs. When she walked to the front where John Lambert sat in the pilot's chair, he opened his eyes, smiled. "Mirtin," he said. "I thought I was the only one who couldn't sleep."

Mirtin ran her fingers through her hair, wished for a comb. "I slept, but not very peaceful."

Lambert chuckled. "I can't remember the last time I had a peaceful sleep. A thousand years ago, perhaps."

Smiling, Mirtin sank into the co-pilot's seat. "I'm surprised you can joke about it. The thousand years, I mean. I can't even imagine how it must be for you, everything and everybody you knew is long gone."

Lambert looked at her, but his eyes didn't seem to see her. "We were just beginning to tame the planets of Alpha Centauri, the closest star-system to Earth that had planets. There was a colony on the fourth planet of Sirius, but it wasn't doing too well. When we left the Solar-System on one of the Seed-Ships, I knew that it would be years for me to get back home, but I never expected this."

Mirtin sat silent for a moment. Her thoughts took her back to a time when Earth, to her, had been nothing but a place where Humanity originated. A place far away from her world. The Enemy. Not really that important. To be watched, but not to be taken seriously, not anymore.

Now here was a man to whom Earth had been the center of known space. He knew nothing of the over hundred colonized star-systems, probably couldn't even fathom the diversity of human life that existed now on the hundreds of populated planets.

She didn't know anything about the world he had lived in, except for the things she learned in school. Very little, when it came to the history of Earth, or even the Solar System.

Humans came to *Liberty,* her home-planet, more than five hundred years ago. Liberty possessed a history colorful enough, why learn about other planets, especially Earth.

She gave Lambert a sidelong glance. He didn't look much different from the people on most other planets. He made love the same way men from her time did. His penis hadn't felt any different inside her.

Thinking about it, she felt suddenly horny.

"I had a dream about my father last night," she said. "We had sexual intercourse."

He looked at her. "Did you?" he asked.

"You mean in real life? Don't be stupid! My father was not that sort of a man. What do you think it means?"

Lambert shrugged. "I'm not a psychologist."

"He changed in my dream, turned into a monstrous creature." She shuddered. "I was captured by them. Viran called them *Zombs*."

"Zombs?"

"Apparently all Xandra-born eventually turn into Zombs."

"I didn't know. By the way, what year is this?"

Mirtin screwed up her eyes. "I guess you want to know the Standard Year. Let me think. 3985 if I'm not mistaken. I don't know the month."

"So you're still using the Earth-calendar?"

Mirtin shook her head. "Only in space. It never occurred to me it might be an Earth-calendar. Every planet has a different year, different seasons. It depends how long it takes for it to circle its Primary."

"Makes sense. I was born on a moon. We had no seasons, every day was the same, but I know about seasons. I've never been on a planet before." His eyes were thoughtful. "What is it like in the year 3985?"

Shrugging, Mirtin said, "Every planet is different. Some societies are moving forward, others like to keep things the same, and they don't want change. There are factions on my own planet who are against any exploration of space."

"How many planets have been colonized? Are they all communicating with each other? They must be spread quite far apart. How do you travel between them? What kind of star-drive are you using?"

Laughing, Mirtin held up her hands. "Slow down, so many questions at once. Unfortunately, my knowledge is limited when it comes to other planetary systems. There are three important powers, the *Solar-Union*--which includes Earth and all the planets in the Solar System, including the moons--, the *Alliance of Independent Planets*, and the *Mandarin Empire*. The rest of the colonized planets are not organized."

"All those planets! Why the interest in this particular one?"

"Your commander asked me this question already. I can't tell you more than I already told him. This planet is unique. We discovered an alien entity here that could be a threat to the whole of humanity. It could also become a powerful ally."

"Against whom?"

"Against the other two powers."

"Whom do you fear? Earth?"

"Earth is no threat. We fear the Mandarin Empire."

Lambert closed his eyes for moment. Mirtin studied him silently, respected his need for reflection. His world gone, where lay his loyalties? Earth? Not necessarily. The military power he had served no longer existed.

"Why do you fear the Mandarin Empire?" he asked. His eyes were still closed.

"The Empire is a military society. It spans across eleven star-systems, 27 planets altogether. There is only one race--no other races are tolerated. Different people had already colonized some of the planets that the Empire invaded. They were either killed or used as slaves."

"Doesn't seem like much has changed." Lambert sounded almost resigned. "You said the Mandarin Empire owns 27 planets. How large is the Alliance?"

"Be careful what you tell him, Captain."

Mirtin turned to look at Massater. "He deserves an answer," she said. "I don't see the harm."

Massater laughed dryly. "You can't be that naive, Lt. Koyo. What do you know about him? Space marine Lambert--explain to me how you can speak the language of the planet Liberty so fluently, without even the slightest accent?"

"The language I speak is English," Lambert answered.

"Well, Lt. Koya and you have conversed in the language that is spoken on her planet, and it is not what you call English."

Mirtin had not been consciously aware that she had spoken in her native language, instead of Inglo-Standard. She stared at Lambert. "I guess an explanation is in order."

"It's the translator behind my ear. A gift from the Genaar."

"The Genaar. I am curious about them." Massater left his seat. "Your commander told me that these aliens have been here for two thousand years. What are they doing here? Where do they come from? Maybe we should worry about them! Can you enlighten me, Marine?"

"I can't tell you anything about the Genaar."

"Can't or won't?" Massater loomed over Lambert. "Who will you chose, Lambert? Humans or your new allies?"

"Take it easy, Colonel," Mirtin spoke up. "John Lambert is not on trial here."

"Sorry." Massater stepped back, wiped his brow. "The Genaar are the first advanced alien race we have encountered. Are they friend or foe?"

"Like you said yourself, they've been here for two thousand years. There are not many of them on the station. I don't believe you have anything to fear from them." Lambert stood up, walked to one of the small screens and adjusted a setting.

Mirtin looked at the screen. It displayed a dirt road, still in darkness, the road where the wagon train would come. Lambert had installed a remote camera and a transmitter in one of the trees. The shuttle was hidden inside a small clearing among dense brush and tall, broad trees, not far from the road, but invisible to anyone who would be coming down the road.

They didn't expect the wagon train to arrive for at least three days, if things went well.

"This alien woman, her name is Starmote, isn't it?" Mirtin asked.

Lambert nodded. "What about her?"

"She used weapons that are superior to what we have. I didn't even know she was armed when she played her little charade; I mean--she was naked for all I could see."

"The Genaar are a very advanced race, and an old one. They may possess a superior technology, but they are not aggressive."

"So they say." Massater chuckled dryly. "She killed a number of men, and you call that *not aggressive*?"

"She acted in self-defense," Lambert said, becoming irritated. "Look, Colonel. We don't really know them, all right? All the men and women on the station are very gentle people. They've never shown any aggression toward us. Starmote, well, she is a little different. She's a soldier."

"Trained to kill," Massater said. "So they can be aggressive, if need be."

Lambert couldn't hide his irritation and showed it when he spoke sharply. "Colonel Massater, what is it you are worried about? There are only fifty aliens on board of the station. Even if aggressive--they are no threat. Without them, we'd be dead a thousand years. As far as I'm concerned, they are our friends, and Starmote has proven her loyalty to Commander Beringer. So, if you don't mind, I'd like to drop the subject."

"Don't be annoyed with the Colonel, John," Mirtin said soothingly. "He has spent a long time in this hell, and in a very hostile environment. I've been here long enough to know what he went through. There is something that bothers me, too. Remember the alien girls, those nymphs, back in Sanctuary? You seem to have been quite fond of one of them." Mirtin blushed a little when she remembered the night by the pond, most of it not very clear, but enough remained.

Lambert smiled, his eyes softened. "Yes. Virni. How can I forget her," he said quietly.

"Didn't the similarity between Starmote and those Nymphs strike you as odd?" Mirtin asked.

"You are absolutely right," Massater agreed. "This alien female looks exactly like a water-nymph. That cannot be just a coincidence."

"I am not going to jump to any conclusions. Maybe there is a connection, I don't know. I'm not a scientist." Lambert gave Mirtin a thoughtful look, then he said slowly, "A thousand years ago we came here with a shipload full of colonists. The humans living on this planet are the descendants of those colonists. The Genaar have been here longer than that. They tried to colonize the planet, but failed. At least that is what we have been told. Maybe they were partially successful." He lifted one shoulder. "I don't know. Our team came down here to find out what happened. The answers may lie in the City."

"Why this particular city? There are others." Mirtin said.

"You've seen them?"

"Only from space, on a viewing screen."

"Back in Sanctuary," Lambert said, "we never did get to finish our conversation. I gather you've been here for some time. I remember you telling me that you came on a rescue-mission." He glanced at Massater. "For the Colonel?"

Mirtin nodded. "He's the reason I am here. Part of the reason, anyway."

"What happened to your ship? Where is the rest of the team?"

"The rest of the team is dead. Our Lander was shot down. We didn't know that the Mandarin Empire had an observation post set up in the mountains. We detected their missile too late. Luckily, they didn't use a self-aware missile, otherwise I would not be sitting here."

"Your Lander was hit?"

"Damaged beyond repair. We crashed in the deepest jungle I've ever seen. The pilot and two of the others were killed on impact. Only four of us got out alive before the Lander exploded."

"There is only you and Vienne," Lambert said.

"Science Officer Monet succumbed to the injuries he sustained in the crash. Lt. Menati was crushed and eaten by a giant snake." Mirtin shuddered, remembering. "Our first encounter with the local wildlife. The snake dropped out of a tree, right in front of Menati. It coiled itself around the lieutenant with such incredible speed that we had no time to react. He was crushed like a soft, ripe fruit. Never had a chance."

"How do you know it was an outpost of the Empire?" Lambert asked.

"Who else? There is nobody else, unless your friends haven't been telling you everything."

"They wouldn't use missiles," Lambert said, defensively. "And they wouldn't have fired the first shot."

"Why don't you give marine Lambert the strategic positions of our defense system, while you're at it, Captain Koyo?" Massater's voice dripped with sarcasm.

Mirtin shot him a venomous glance. The man began to annoy her, but she suppressed the urge to scream at him. Her nerves were raw, and the close confinement of the ancient shuttle made her claustrophobic. She needed some fresh air. "I'm going outside," she announced, "the air in here is getting stale."

"It is not advisable. Not until daylight," Lambert said.

"Is there any danger lurking out there? I'm sure your primitive instruments can detect that?" When she saw Lambert lift his eyebrows, she said, "I'm sorry. I know you're concerned about my safety, but I just have to get out."

"I'm coming with you," Vienne, who had been silent until now, got out of her seat.

"I thought your were sleeping," Mirtin said.

"I was, until everybody started yelling."

Lambert told the shuttle's computer to open the exit. The door slid open. Humid, cool air entered the cabin. It smelled of decaying leaves and some other, quite familiar fragrance. Mirtin glanced at Lambert. His young face looked suddenly flushed, his breath seemed to come a little faster. When he looked at her, she knew what went through his mind. Maybe it wasn't such a good idea to go outside. Shrugging, she stepped through the opening and climbed down the steps.

Through the branches, she could see one of the moons, the red one. Someone else came down the steps, when she turned she saw Vienne.

The blond girl took a deep breath, looked up at the red moon. "I don't like it here, Mirtin," she said softly. "I'm completely screwed up.

I keep thinking of that savage, Viran, how he felt inside me. I…I want to experience that again, with a man. Any man."

Mirtin smiled and put her arms around the younger girl. "There is nothing to be ashamed of. I want the same thing. Right now, as a matter of fact." She breathed deeply, inhaled the fragrance in the air. She knew if she started looking, somewhere nearby she would find a bed of purple flowers.

Both girls turned, startled by the harsh drumming of a night-creature, then a high-pitched scream, not of fright, but a challenge. Mirtin felt Vienne tremble when they heard the flapping sound of a pair of giant wings. "Let's go back inside," she said. "I don't feel safe out here."

When she climbed up the steps, she turned around, looked back at the dark trees. For a moment, she thought she saw shadows moving between the massive trunks. Shrugging, she entered the shuttle, cursing silently for feeling so jittery.

Chapter Nine

Viran looked down at the pile of bones. They were fresh. Broken and splintered, crushed between strong teeth, but still recognizable as human. All the skulls had been cracked open, the brain scooped out of their cavity.

"I feel guilty," he said to Tegron.

The big man shook his head. "Why should you?"

"We should have left them some weapons."

"Did you forget what they did? They murdered those angels thoughtlessly, and with malice. They deserved to die."

"Not like this, ripped apart alive and eaten by scavengers. A man should only die in battle, or of old age."

Tegron laughed. "You can be assured, these died in battle."

"You are so different from any Xandra-born I've ever met. I was told the children of the Great Mother are all docile and non-violent. Yet--you killed some men today, and you show no pity for the ones who died such a violent death. You could almost be a True-Human."

"I was once," Tegron said. "A long time ago. I used to be a mercenary, selling my sword-arm to anyone willing to pay for my services. I was wild and I thought I'd never grow old, but I did. One day I was an old man, sick and dying of an old man's disease, unable to even move. Mercenaries have no friends, but my companions took pity on me and sacrificed me to the Xandra. She absorbed my old body, and then she created a new one, with all my memories intact." Tegron looked at Viran. "The Great Mother gave a lot of herself to repair your damaged body. So you see, you and I are a lot closer than you thought, my brother."

"But I am still a True-Human," Viran said. Then he smiled, gave his new friend a slap on the back. "We'd better move on. I don't want to spend another night in the open." He looked back the way they came. The tracks from their horses were clearly visible in the soft soil, but already the heat of the morning sun dried out the ground, and the trampled grass began to straighten out.

The night had not been pleasant. Huddled among the protecting tangled roots of the Ocla-tree, he slept very little. His blanket was still wet from the night's rain. He thought of Horgan and the rest of his companions. By now, their ship should have reached the island, after battling the hostile sea. When he closed his eyes, he could feel the icy wind on his skin and taste the salty water, as it splashed over his face.

Would he ever set foot on a ship again? Would he ever again climb the giant boulders that covered the plains of his island, hunting the fierce one-horned Rock-bulls? He thought of his mother, Helegar. She must think him dead. How could she think otherwise, since he had not returned with the team?

"Are you falling asleep on top of your horse?"

Viran opened his eyes, gave Tegron a rueful smile. "I was thinking about my mother. I wish I could let her know that I'm alive."

"She is important to you?"

"She is my mother. When my father was killed, it was left to me to take care of her. I'm her only son."

"Is she beautiful?"

Viran smiled. "Every mother is beautiful."

"She'll find a man to protect her," Tegron said with conviction. "Women are skilled at that. Come, let's go."

They rode on in silence. Wild Spirit moved powerfully underneath Viran, carrying him on his broad back with apparent ease. Traveling seemed easier today, Viran had adjusted himself to the gait of the big horse.

At midday, they stopped beside a fast flowing brook to water the animals and give them some rest.

Viran slid off Wild Spirit, his legs stiff and his back sore. Stretching, he grinned at Tegron who didn't seem to suffer the same discomfort. "I think you were born on the back of a horse," he said.

Tegron laughed. "Not exactly, but I've spent most of my life in the company of horses. They are good companions, dependable and loyal." He led his steed toward the brook and lay flat on his belly beside the horse to drink from the clear water.

Viran followed his example. He drank sparingly, even though his throat was parched. After splashing cold water on his neck and face, he decided to submerge his whole body into the cooling liquid. Shedding his clothes, he jumped naked into the water, discovering it colder than he'd thought, but still a welcome relief from the burning heat of the sun.

Tegron joined him and laughing like two boys, they began splashing each other.

"I thought you were an old man," Viran laughed when they lay on their backs in the high grass, soaking up the sun's warming rays.

"Your true self never gets old," Tegron replied, "only your body. But this body is young."

"When were you… ah… born?"

"Ten summers ago. As you see, I'm still a child."

In the late afternoon, they arrived at the river, traveled along a well-used road. They decided to take one of the side-roads in search of a place to spend the night, hoping to find a farmhouse.

They did, except it looked abandoned. They passed two ponds and found evidence of violence in the form of destroyed seedpods and floating pieces of a Xandra-plant. The farmhouse was large, a two-story building with big windows and many rooms inside.

"There were people here only recently," Viran said. "They must have left in a hurry."

On the wooden table in the kitchen stood plates with leftover food. Tegron smelled it. "Just a few days old," he said.

"Maybe we'll find some smoked meat." Viran searched and found the door that led into the cellar. He climbed down the ladder and came back shortly, carrying two large sausages and a flask of wine. "There is more," he said. "We can replenish our supplies."

Tegron found some biscuits in one of the cupboards and they sat down to consume an unexpected and enjoyable meal.

"Life cannot get any better," Tegron grinned and took another swig of wine.

"You are right," Viran agreed. "I can think only of one thing that would top this."

"What would that be, my brother?"

"A woman. A beautiful, willing woman."

"Ahh." Tegron wiped his mouth. Stroking his mustache, he stared at the dancing flames of the oil lamp on the table. "I've known many beautiful women and shared their bed." He chuckled. "Some ugly ones, too."

Viran leaned forward and squinted at his companion. The wine began to have its effect on him. "Tell me, do you still feel the urge to couple with a woman?"

"Why shouldn't I?"

"Because Xandra-born cannot reproduce like True-Humans. What reason would there be?"

"Pleasure. Besides, as I told you, I am not truly Xandra-born. Before this new body, I did father a few children. Not because I wanted to, but because the women thought I might stay if they gave me a child.

And I did give my fare share of seeds to the Xandra. Even though I couple only for pleasure now, I still remember the real reason why a man and a woman join their bodies." He pointed a finger at Viran. "I am still a man, just so you know. I have bedded quite a few True-Human women since my rebirth and enjoyed their uncontrolled passion. They gave themselves to me completely, because they knew that coupling with me would produce no offspring."

Viran cocked his head and stared at the door, listening. "Did you hear that?" he asked.

This time both of them heard the light pounding. Viran jumped to his feet and staggered toward the door, shaking his head to clear it. In his hand, he held his unsheathed knife. He opened the door, stepped back and peered outside.

Standing in the doorway, framed against the rising moon, stood a woman, naked, and quite beautiful. She carried a large gourd. "We thought you might need some company," she said, smiling, and stepped into the room. Behind her came two more women, as beautiful and naked as the first one.

"We brought some wine." She put the gourd on the table.

She was tall and slim; her breasts not large, but beautifully shaped, with long thick nipples. Her black thick hair hung down to her buttocks. Viran noticed the thick curly mat of her pubic hair below her flat belly.

One of the other two women stepped closer to Viran and offered her gourd. "Here, drink," she said with a sultry voice. Viran looked into her eyes and registered their strange, yellow-flecked color and the tiny black pupils. He took the offered gourd and put it to his lips. The wine tasted sweet and fruity.

How much he drank, he didn't remember. Someone pulled down his pants. He found himself kneeling behind one of the women, her buttocks looming high in front of him. He could see the pink of her sex-organ between her white, plump cheeks. A soft hand curled around his penis, another one pushed him gently forward.

He watched in fascination as his stiff penis touched the pink orifice of the woman kneeling in front of him. Another push and then he slid into creamy softness. His hands grabbed the woman's hips and he began to move in and out of her. Soft breasts flattened against his back, a warm body molded itself to him, moved with him.

The woman kneeling in front of him turned her head; her yellow eyes looked feral as she arched her back to take him deeper into her. He came with a loud grunt; his penis pumped its precious liquid into the woman's greedily sucking organ.

Then she slipped out of his grasp, but another one took her place, her fleshy buttocks up to receive him. Still stiff, he entered the beckoning pink cleft with a moan and slid into the hot interior.

The woman behind him moved to his side, kissed him hungrily. "Have some more wine," she whispered into his ear. He shook his head, knowing he drank too much already.

"Enough wine!" he said hoarsely, slamming his belly into soft buttocks. He didn't even remember having climaxed, and he was determined to be aware of it when it happened this time. His fingers grabbed the long, thick hair of the woman he coupled with, and pulled back her head. He bent forward, cupped her slim body and kissed her on the mouth. Her lips opened and her tongue slid into his mouth. Even in his befuddled state, he noticed the unusual length of her tongue.

Feeling his orgasm approaching, he clamped his hands around the woman's rotating hips, held her tight, pushed deep and let go. His penis felt huge inside her tight channel, pleasure surged through his body as he shot his discharge into her.

Looking back at him with bright, yellow eyes, the woman growled deep in her throat as she received his seeds. After he finished, she moved forward and freed his still stiff mast.

When the third woman knelt down, he grabbed her and put her onto her back. She struggled, but then she opened her legs wide to let him lie between them. He found her as ready as the other two, her channel hot and moist. Soft walls closed around his pole as he entered her. "Tell me when you are ready," she whispered. He nodded and began to slide in and out of her. She moaned softly, moved against him with an unexpected, but welcome ferociousness.

Slamming his own body into hers, for a moment afraid of hurting her, he need not have worried. She wrapped her long legs around his and crushed him to her. When he felt his climax approaching, he told her so. She stopped moving and pushed him off with surprising strength. Then she knelt in front of him. "Put it back in," she said urgently, her breath coming fast. He spread her white cheeks, pushed his pole back into her steaming sex-organ. She growled and began milking him.

Now!" he called out and pushed deep into her. As his penis gushed, the outlines of her body seemed to blur, her body changed. Coarse, black hair sprouted from her skin, and before he finished, he found his spurting organ buried inside the sex-organ of a hairy creature with a long snout, filled with sharp, pointy teeth.

The creature's head turned and looked back at him with large gold flecked eyes. A long tongue lolled between those sharp teeth. He could hear the creature's labored breathing.

Not finished with his climax, he held on tight to the narrow hairy hips in his grasp until the throbbing in his penis subsided, then he let go and pulled out of the incredibly tight sheath that held him prisoner.

He'd never seen one of these creatures before, but he knew of them. His people called them *Were-hounds*. She was a female *Were-hound*.

A *Were-woman*.

The males of her species were not capable of reproducing, so the females took on human form and mated with human males. After receiving a man's sperm, the female had to change back into her natural form, preferably at the same instant as the seeds entered her womb.

Copulating with the last of the Were-Women had sapped his strength. He fell to his side and lay there, chest heaving, his breath coming in short gasps. Through the window fell pale light, when he looked up, he saw the full disk of one the two Wanderers, partially obscured by the branches of the trees. Then he heard barking sounds and the howling of a lone Were-hound. Another one joined in and soon a whole pack of them howled outside the house.

A shadow blocked the light from the window. Outlined against the pale light stood a naked man, coarse hair matted his broad chest and belly. "You have served my bitches well," he said with a deep, gravelly voice. "Did they please you in return?"

"I am satisfied," Viran murmured. His brain only slowly reacting to the man's presence. There must have been something in the wine to dull his senses.

The man crouched beside him, held a flask against Viran's lips. "Here, drink this, it will return your strength."

Viran looked into the man's yellow eyes. He didn't sense any menace from him, but he knew he could be in danger. He drank from the offered flask, swallowed the bitter liquid and let it run down his throat.

"There is one more favor I ask of you." The man smiled.

Viran stared at the long incisors in the man's mouth. "What is it you want me to do?" Viran asked, his voice not as slurry anymore. He could feel the fog lifting from his brain. His hand went to his hip, but he didn't find the knife he groped for.

"Nothing you won't enjoy." The man stood up and pointed at the open door. Within its frame stood a young woman, a girl really, barely past puberty. Her long black hair hung like a veil across her face. When she moved, her hair parted. The flickering light from the oil lamp reflected momentarily in her golden eyes.

"This young bitch has not been bred, yet," the man said. "She has entered her first heat-cycle. I want you to impregnate her, but be warned, she is wild."

Viran looked at the slim naked form of the girl. Her budding breasts were small, her hips not flaring, like that of a mature woman. Even her genitals were barely covered with dark curly hair. She opened her mouth to display tiny fangs. A soft growl came from her throat. Rotating her slim hips, she stared at him in defiance.

"I'll impregnate your virgin," Viran said, feeling his mast rising between his legs.

The man laughed. "I didn't say she was a virgin. I just said she hasn't been bred, yet--by a human."

The girl moved closer. She stood above him, her legs planted on either side of his body. He could see the creamy drops of fluid coming out of her bright pink cleft. The puffy lips were quivering with anticipation. This young bitch was ready.

She sank into his lap, impaled herself on his rigid mast, all in one fluid movement. He slid easily into her warm, greasy sheath. Snapping her slim hips back and forth, she rode him with powerful, ferocious strokes. She threw back her head, howled against the moon still visible through the window.

Suddenly there were other females beside her. They were older, their hair almost white. Grabbing the girl, they pulled her off Viran. She fought them by snapping at them, but they were strong enough to dislodge her. Then they forced her to kneel and pushed her head down.

Viran got into position behind her and let one of the females guide his stiff organ. With a loud grunt, he entered the young Were-girl's tight sheath and moved forcefully between her small, round buttocks. She bucked and howled, and when he exploded inside her, she pushed back against him, tightening the walls of her vagina with crushing force around his spurting organ.

The outlines of her form shimmered, changed and soon sleek dark fur covered her body. Her head flattened, lost its human shape. Yellow eyes looked back at him; long fangs gleamed in the moonlight.

He held her until his climax subsided. Her tight grip on his penis never lessened. It became even tighter after she assumed animal shape.

She snapped at the two older women who held her, but they didn't let go. Viran kept moving back and forth, sliding in and out of the young female Were-hound's tight sheath, his penis still stiff and hard.

Again, her body began to change, the fur receded, and long hair grew from her rounded skull. He dug his fingers into the girl's white, soft hips, bent over her to cup her small body. His hands closed over her budding young breasts, squeezed them gently, his fingers fondling the long nipples. She arched her back and sucked greedily on his rampant penis. With great force he hammered his hips against her small buttocks, feeling her inner muscles rippling along his rigid shaft.

She bucked, then howled. He knew he didn't cause her any pain.

The two older women let go of her, giving her freedom to move as she pleased. Her tight channel milked him with ever-increasing speed, faster and faster. Someone pushed the spout of a gourd into his mouth and he drank from the welcome sweet nectar. Strength flowed through his veins and he moved with renewed vigor. As the lead Were-Hound had said, the girl was wild, demanding all his strength. After climaxing so many times, it took Viran a long time to come again. When he felt his orgasm approaching, he knew it would be a huge one. Waiting as long as he could, he finally couldn't hold back any longer. His roar of pleasure blended with the girl's howls as he filled her young womb.

Her body changed back into her natural form. When his penis lost its rigidity, she relaxed her grip on him and let him pull out of her. She stood docile, looked up at the two women who stroked her head

Both of the women fell to their knees, their bodies changed and took on animal form. Viran watched them pad out of the door. The young female hound threw one last look at him before she slipped into the night.

Viran closed his eyes, listened to the howls of the pack prowling around the house.

Not seeing Tegron anywhere, he wondered what happened to him. He became aware of soft growling sounds in one of the rooms. Pushing open the door, he saw Tegron kneeling behind one of the white-haired women, pounding his lean belly forcefully into her fleshy buttocks. As Viran watched, Tegron stiffened, pulled the woman into is lap and held her tight. His buttocks quivered and the woman's belly rippled furiously.

Tegron let go, the woman moved forward, changed into a hound. She bared sharp teeth when she looked at Viran, then she slipped by him and joined the rest of her pack outside.

Tegron grinned at Viran. "Even the old bitches still enjoy coupling with a man, preferably a man like me. The last thing they want is another pup."

Viran felt suddenly very tired. "I need some rest," he said. Walking back to lock the outside-door, he saw that it stood wide open.

Looking into the night, he stared in surprise at the figure standing on the steps.

Chapter Ten

The ship rocked gently in the rolling waves. They'd have to spend another night in the bay before setting out to sea. She was a good ship, strong and sturdy, but they'd be foolish to brave the waters now. It would take more than the rest of the day to reach the open sea and relative safety from the breakers that punished the rocky entrance to the bay.

Old Grisgaar watched the last of the teams push their boat into the water. One day late, but at least they made it. The other four teams had arrived within the last two days, each of them loaded with the supplies needed on the island.

He saw the bulky shape of Horgan pacing back and forth among the rocks on shore and he could almost hear him roaring his commands as his team-members loaded up the boat.

The boat sat low in the water, loaded with men and supplies. Sometimes it disappeared from view as it fought its way through the foamy whitecaps. Wet and cursing, the men finally climbed up the rope ladder, while the men on board pulled up the full and heavy baskets.

Old Grisgaar counted the men, who clambered over the wooden railing, discovered one missing. Looking over the tired young warriors, he knew who. A lump formed in his belly as he bent over the railing to see if he still lingered in the boat.

"Where is Viran?" he asked Horgan, the team-leader.

The old warrior stayed silent for a moment, then his big hand clamped over Grisgaar's shoulder.

"We lost him," Horgan said hoarsely.

"Dead?"

Horgan shrugged. "We were summoned. In the morning, his war-hammer was still there, but he was gone. We couldn't wait, you know the law."

"You never saw his body?" Hope surged through Old Grisgaar. How could he explain it to Helegar, his brother's widow, Viran's mother?

Horgan shook his head.

He looks tired, worn out, Grisgaar thought. His time has come. The team needed a new leader. Viran would have been the natural choice.

Viran differed from the other young men his age. Not only was he big and strong, but also smart and good-natured, not hotheaded, like Avaro and Kormic. And a born leader, like his father before him.

Grisgaar's hands gripped the railing, squeezed until his knuckles were white. Gritting his teeth, he spat into the angry water, trying to fight back the tears that stung his eyes.

When he turned, Horgan was gone. The old warrior could not be blamed. Two of the other teams lost a man each. One, young Brisl, had stumbled into a *Wolf-Spider's* web, and the other one, Volca, a seasoned warrior, died in battle when his team walked into the camp of slave-traders.

The world was a violent place. Men got killed.

But why Viran?

Old Grisgaar stared at the seashore; his eyes searched the rocks and the forest beyond, expecting to see Viran burst into view. When a heavy hand touched his shoulder, he turned to look at the captain of the ship. "Orsin," he said, "is everything alright?"

"He's not coming," Orsin said, his voice raw from shouting commands. His small eyes were hidden behind bushy eyebrows, and his usually red beard streaked white from the saltwater. "He is my sister's son. I am as fond of him as you are. We won't sail till tomorrow, but if you're thinking of leaving the ship to search for him, forget it. I won't loose you, too."

Grisgaar nodded. "I'll go help the youngsters stow away the baskets," he said and began walking across the rolling deck, slippery from the water washing over it and from the previous night's downpour. He reached for one of the thick ropes to catch his balance, fearful of making a fool of himself. A warrior belonged on solid land, not on a flimsy wooden floating hut that could easily provide a quick snack for one of the giant serpents who lived in the ocean. Mind you, nobody he knew had ever seen one, but there were stories.

Bumping his hip into one of the masts, he let out a loud curse. The wound in his side had healed long ago, only the scars remained, but the bones underneath didn't let him forget his last encounter with the Neanders.

I'm getting old, he thought, his feet searching for the rung of the ladder that led below deck. The storage rooms were underneath the living areas, in the bowels of the ship. There was not much room, and Grisgaar had to duck so he wouldn't bump his head against the thick beams in the low ceiling.

Most of the young warriors were already in their narrow bunks, exhausted from their ordeal. He could hear their snoring from the sleeping quarters above. Raul and Deter, two of the warriors from Horgan's team, pushed their baskets into a free spot, nodded to Grisgaar and climbed up the ladder to join the others for some well-deserved rest.

Each of the five teams consisted of four warriors and six carriers. Back on the ship, the carriers also doubled up as deck hands.

Old Grisgaar only came along as an advisor, so Captain Orsin told him, but Grisgaar was no fool. He came along because everyone loved to listen to his stories, and he also happened to be a fair cook, which couldn't be said of Dorgan, the designated ship's cook.

Luckily, the journey usually lasted only nine or ten days, and as long as they had enough wine, stale bread, and salted meat one could get by without ever tasting the gruel Dorgan put on the wooden plates.

In the flickering light of an oil lamp Grisgaar surveyed the goods. The storage room was filled to capacity. It had been a successful mission. Grisgaar saw piles of warm blankets, stacked in one corner. Beside them a basket filled with cooking-pots made from iron, another basket full of long-bladed, rusty, but well-made knifes.

One of the teams obviously met up with a trading caravan and successfully traded for items that could not be manufactured or found on the island.

The people on the island were skilled when it came to making goods from leather, which they processed from the tough skins of the sea-bulls. Sea-bulls made their home in the frigid waters of the north, but in the spring, they came down as far as the island, where they climbed on land to mate.

Besides the skin and the red meat, the eyes were the most prized. Covered by a thick, horny transparent skin, which, when carefully sliced from the eyeball, cleaned and dried, could be used to catch the rays of the sun. Held over a small pile of dried leaves, the leaves would soon catch fire. A handful of sea-bull eyes fetched a great deal of valuable trading goods.

There were many other things found on the island, which could be used for trading. *Diams*, for instance, many faceted, transparent crystals. A shard, jammed between two flat stones tied together, could be used for cutting almost anything. Some of the women pressed them into bracelets, which they made from leather. Otherwise, they weren't worth much, because of their abundance on the island.

Grisgaar examined the baskets Horgan's team stowed away, pleased to see one filled with rare *Blood-leafs*. The medicine-women would be grateful. Some of the children in Grisgaar's village had been infected with the dreaded *Red-spot Disease,* which could only be cured with an infusion made from boiled Blood-leafs. They did not grow on the island, because of the cold. The mountain tribes would pay a good price for a pouch full of leafs.

In one of the other baskets he found a stack of black chewing sticks, highly prized with the men and the women, and not just because of their pain-killing properties. A small piece chewed before going to sleep brought pleasant and erotic dreams, but also gave a man tremendous staying power.

A sudden itch in his crotch made him rub himself. Old Grisgaar grinned, bit off a large chunk of one of the sticks. Right now, he could use a good, willing woman. There was still plenty of juice left in this old warrior.

He suddenly remembered Horgan telling him that the Xandra had summoned his team. It happened sometimes. The Great Mother was in constant need of new seeds and used every opportunity to add to the seed-pool. Even though the people from the island did note worship the Xandra, the men were not above becoming *seed-givers*.

Xandra-born females were incredibly beautiful and very skilled in coupling, or *collecting seeds* as they called it. A man could do worse than joining with one of the Xandra's daughters. No True-Human female could give the level of pleasure that a Xandra-born could give.

And no human woman smelled and tasted as good as the daughters of the Xandra.

Suddenly tired, Old Grisgaar killed the sputtering flame of his oil-lamp and looked in the semi-darkness for a comfortable spot to lie down. He found it in one of the corners and soon he drifted off into a world of dreams, where he was young and handsome, dreamed of a time when he met a beautiful woman with long, flaming red hair.

He spent a night of ecstasy in her embrace. She had taken him to pleasurable heights he didn't know existed. Her mouth, her breasts, and her sex-organ tasted of sweet nectar, which ran down his throat like liquid fire.

It happened a long time ago, but the memory never left him.

Chapter Eleven

Lt. Darrin Chow Wang watched the shuttle disappear above the treetops. He worried about his commander, but he couldn't think of anything he could have done. Behind him the General's tent still smoldered, the reek of burning leather nauseating and unpleasant. Watching a group of soldiers dragging their dead comrades toward the edge of the forest, he sighed and began walking in the direction of the wagons, where Esram and his sons were busy hitching their horses to the wagons.

The old man looked up when he saw Wang approaching. Taking off his grimy wide-brimmed hat, he ran a big-knuckled hand across his bald skull and spat a thick, black wad into the ground. He gave Wang a long, hard look. "That story about you being shipwrecked--I never believed it," he said.

The lieutenant smiled. "The Commander was never a good liar."

"You could have left with your friends."

"I could have." Wang shrugged. "I wanted to make sure you were safe."

When a soft hand touched his elbow, he turned to see one of the Xandra-born girls standing beside him. She brushed a strand of black hair out of her eyes and smiled at him. Behind her dark lashes, her eyes sparkled with green fire. "I am glad you stayed," she said softly.

"Tamsy," he smiled and lost himself in the depth of her green eyes, but only for a moment. *God, she's beautiful,* he thought and tore himself away. This was not the time. "I stayed to protect you," he said, and stroked her hair.

"Thank you," she said with a shy smile. "Will you come to the City with us?"

Wang nodded. "Of course I will. How else could I protect you?" There were other reasons, like their mission to find out as much a possible about this planet, but he didn't tell her.

While talking to Tamsy, Wang kept a watchful eye on a group of soldiers who were milling around the wagons. One of them walked toward them. Wang put his hand on his weapon, ready to draw it from its holster.

The young soldier stopped in front of Esram. "Can I talk to you for a moment, Farmer?"

Esram looked at him, his face clearly hostile. "Talk," he said.

"Not all Amaarins hate the Xandra-born," the young soldier said, hesitatingly. "I don't."

"Then why are you here?"

"Because I had no choice. Anyone who speaks out is executed. Even my family would not be safe." He pointed back at his friends. "I am not alone."

"So what is it you want?" Esram didn't sound convinced.

"We want to join you. With your help we could get to the City to ask the Mother for protection."

"How many of you are there?"

"Five, including myself."

The old man scratched his head. "I'm not sure," he said. "What would prevent you from cutting our throats when we are sleeping, just to take revenge?"

"We are not murderers."

Esram's laugh sounded like a drowning man gasping for air. "I don't trust you, Amaarin. Your people murdered my cousin's family."

The young soldier looked at Wang. "I know nothing about that, I swear. I've never killed anyone, not even a Xandra-born. You are a soldier. I give you my word as a soldier that we will not be a threat to you."

"Why do you want to go to the City so badly?" Wang asked.

"Because I cannot go back home. I will be imprisoned, or even executed."

"Why?"

"My father was sent to prison for speaking out against the *Reverend* and his followers, *The Pure-Ones.* This happened just after I joined the army."

Esram shook his head and murmured, "Lies."

"Not lies, truth!" protested the young soldier.

"How about your friends?" asked Wang.

"They have their own reasons, all of them valid."

The lieutenant studied the young man's face. He seemed anxious and nervous, had a tendency to look at the ground when he talked, but he couldn't detect any malice in the young soldier's behavior. "What's your name?" he asked.

"I am Mirko, and you?"

"My name is Darrin Wang, most people call me Wang."

"So what do you say, Wang?"

The lieutenant shrugged. "It's not really my decision. If Esram says it is alright, I have no objections."

"He speaks the truth," Tamsy said beside Wang.

"How can you be sure?"

Tamsy stood in front of Mirko, looked into his eyes. "We Xandra-born have the ability. We are not easily deceived," she said and looked at Esram. "Let him come with us. The Mother will be pleased."

Esram spit into the dust. "I'm willing to take a chance. We could use a few more hands. Depends what the women have to say."

"Say about what?" Lyra, Esram's wife, came walking up to them. She looked tired and old.

"This young soldier and some of his friends want to join up with us to travel to the City. You might say he is defecting to our side."

Lyra gave Mirko the once-over-look, smiled and said, "He's handsome enough. I have no objections."

Aran, the youngest of the grown sons, stared at the soldier. "I'll be watching you," he said. "If I don't like your behavior I'll put a bullet into your brain, understood?"

Mirko stared back, then he nodded. "I'll tell my friends." He turned and stalked back to his watching companions.

It was almost midday when the wagon train finally left the campsite. Lt. Wang and Stark, one of Esram's sons, rode ahead, scouting the trail. The Amaarin soldiers rode in the rear.

Stark drew rein beside Wang. He was tall and well built, a little older than Aran. A thin mustache adorned his upper lip and from his narrow chin sprouted a small goatee. "I don't trust them," he told Wang.

"Tamsy thinks they're alright," Wang said. "I'm inclined to believe her."

"The Xandra-born can be a bit naive, sometimes. They are like children, not too smart. They trust everybody."

Wang smiled. "I don't know much about Tamsy's people, but you are right, she is very child-like. We'll keep an eye on our guests." He looked into the cloudless sky. It promised to be a warm, dry day. The road the traveled on appeared solid, they should be able to cover a good distance.

"Are you hungry?" Stark asked him.

"Not really." Wang ate one of his ration-packs. Not a very tasty meal, but nourishing.

"I'm starved," Stark said. "I'll see if I can get some biscuits."

He fell back, waited for the first wagon to catch up with him.

Wang spotted movement ahead. A lone rider stood in the middle of the road, two huge hounds beside him. Wang loosened the gun in his holster and pulled out his far-lenses. Zooming in on the rider, he recognized him.

Robar, Esram's oldest son.

The hounds were the first to come bounding down the road, followed a little slower by Robar. Amaar, who rode behind Wang, jumped from his horse, greeted the hounds with open arms. The first one jumped on him, bowling him over. Both, man and beast rolled on the ground like two children. Laughing, Amaar told the hound to calm down, but the big animal kept licking his face. Amaar finally managed to get to his feet. Still laughing, he dusted himself off. "He's just a big puppy," he said to Wang.

Wang remembered the incident at the Ballard-Farm and shuddered slightly. The smell of human blood and ripped-out entrails still lingering in his nose.

Robar reached them with a huge grin. "You don't know how happy I am to see you," he said to his younger brother. "Is everybody alright?"

"We are fine--now. We worried about you, big brother." Amar gave Robar a hug and clapped him on the back.

From one of the wagons came a loud cry. When Wang looked, he saw Mirna jumping to the ground, then she came running, crying out Robar's name. Robar caught her in his arms, lifting her into the air. She covered his face with kisses. "Easy, little sister." Robar pushed her away, laughing.

"We thought you were dead," she sobbed.

He laughed. "As you can see, I am very much alive."

In the meantime, old Esram and Lyra had climbed off their wagon. Esram blew his nose, spit a black wad into the dirt. Then he took off his wide-brimmed hat and wiped his eyes with his sleeves. "So you managed to elude those soldiers," he rumbled and padded the big head of one of the hounds. "I'm glad to see the hounds are still alive."

Robar grinned and gave his father a hug. "I worried about you, too," he said. "All of you. How did you get away?"

Before anyone could answer, he whirled and bent to pick up his rifle, which he had dropped to the ground. He lifted it to his cheek. "Amaarins," he growled.

"They are with us," Esram said.

Without lowering his weapon, Robar asked, "Are you their prisoner?"

"No, they want to go to the City with us."

"They are deserters," Aran said.

Robar let his rifle drop, but kept his eyes on the riders who stopped their horses behind the last wagon. "Deserters, hmm…"

"There are only five of them," Mirna said, "and they seem to be nice."

Lyra, who hadn't said a word until now, walked quietly up to her son and pulled him toward her. Holding him for a moment, she lifted up on her toes and planted a kiss on his nose. "There has been enough bloodshed," she said and brushed a tear out of her eye. "The ones who murdered your father's cousin and her family have been punished. These young men asked for our help, we can't turn them down."

"What about Quirma, or Helgie? How do they feel about having Amaarin butchers in our midst?" Robar cursed under his breath. "I don't like it."

"These boys had nothing to do with the murders. They are victims, too." Mirna put her hand on her brother's arm. "When I saw Keltie and little Corba lying in their blood I was consumed with anger. I wanted nothing but revenge, but Mother is right, we must not condemn all of the Amaarins."

Robar's eyes softened, he stroked Mirna's hair, then he bent and kissed her on the mouth. "My little sister," he said, "you are not always this forgiving. Are you sure you have no ulterior motive?"

The young girl blushed and stared at the group of Amaarin soldiers who sat on their horses, watching. One of them, Mirko, saw her looking, smiled, and then touched his chest with his left hand in a quick salute.

Robar snorted. "You have one child already, because you couldn't keep your legs crossed, little sister. You don't want another one, so soon."

Mirna pouted. "Don't be angry with me, big brother, we've been through this before. I know, you never approved of my marriage to Rolard, but I love him, and he loves me." She pushed out her breasts. "Besides, I am not a little girl anymore. I'm a woman now."

The crying of a child made Rolar smile. "I'm sorry; I didn't mean to upset you. It is just because I love you and care for you. You better look after your son; he's calling for his mother."

"Don't always criticize her," Lyra said as Mirna walked away. "She may be a mother, but she is still a little girl, easily hurt. You know that she adores you." She looked at the soldiers. "Besides, a little new blood wouldn't hurt," she mused, then she laughed. "Just kidding."

Robar looked around. "What happened to the other two hounds?"

Esram cursed loudly, spit into the dust. "The Amaarins shot them. I couldn't prevent it."

"Too bad, they were good animals."

"Better them than one of us." The old man looked at Lt. Wang. "Do you have a family?" he asked.

Wang hesitated, remembering, then he shook his head. "Not anymore," he said, a pang of regret stabbing him like a sharp knife.

"Maybe some day you'll have one of your own. It can be a burden, sometimes." He walked away, stiffly, back to the wagon.

Lyra looked after him and smiled. "He loves his family, even if he won't admit it. Come, Robar, lead us to safety. It'll be dark soon and it would be good to be out of the forest by nightfall. I don't trust the night-creatures. There are large bands of Neanders roaming this part of the forest; we don't want to encounter them."

Wang joined Robar, Stark, and Aran in the front. Elia and Oran, the other two sons, rode in the rear, with the soldiers.

Darkness already closed in when they finally left the forest, but they didn't have far to travel to find a good campsite. This was not the first time that Esram and his family made the trek to the City. They were quite familiar with the road and with what they might encounter. Seeking protection from the high winds that sometimes blew across the open land, they made camp inside a small grove of trees. A spring-fed pond supplied them with good, clean water.

It didn't surprise Wang when he saw the, by now familiar, Xandra-plant floating in the pond. A batch of purple flowers grew to one side. Their intoxicating fragrance was the first thing Wang became aware of as he stiffly dismounted from his steed. He felt the gentle stirring in his loins, but ignored it, deciding not to follow his impulse to push the nose-filter in place. He could control the urges the scent of the flowers invoked.

The Xandra-girls pitched their small tents beside the pond. Esram and his family erected only one large tent for the women. The men preferred to sleep in the open, rolled into their blankets. The young Amaarin soldiers set up their camp on the other side of the pond, away from the others. They seemed to be as apprehensive as Esram's family.

One of the sons, Oran, made a fire, and his brother Elia cut down some branches from one of the trees to build a tripod for the large cooking pot. It didn't take long before Lyra took over and began cooking a hearty stew.

Mirna insisted that they invite the young soldiers. They accepted, somewhat reluctant, but they had been given a show of good will and were smart enough to take advantage of it. At first conversations were cool, but after Esram served some of his wine, the atmosphere became warmer and even Robar, who seemed the most hostile, exchanged a few words with one of the Amaarins.

After supper, Tamsy snuggled up beside Wang. She didn't say anything, just seemed content to listen to the conversations of the True-Humans. When time came to go to sleep, Tamsy stayed with Wang. He didn't mind, especially since she brought a couple of blankets. "You could sleep inside one of the tents, where you would not be bothered by the *cricks,*" Wang said.

Tamsy laughed. "They only bother True-Humans. They don't like Xandra-blood."

Cricks were small insects that came out a night, and they gave nasty bites. The milliwave-generator strapped to Wang's wrist repulsed them, most of the time.

Wang felt tired, his backside sore from spending much of the day on horseback. Sensing his discomfort, Tamsy was content just to lie in his arms.

How long he slept, he didn't know. A weight on his chest awoke him. Opening his eyes, he looked into Tamsy's smiling face; the light of the two moons, which had risen into the sky, reflected from her green eyes.

"What are you doing?" he whispered.

She giggled. "You must ask?" she whispered back.

The scent of the Xandra-flowers hung strong in the air. He became aware of his penis pushing hard against the fabric of his pants. Wriggling her hips, Tamsy kissed him passionately. When they broke apart for air, he said, "Not here, Tamsy. Let's go to the other side of the pond, at least."

"Alright, go ahead, I'll go and collect a seed-pouch." She slipped out of her cotton-dress. Naked, she ran toward the pond and dove gracefully into it.

Wang walked as quietly as he could among the trees, away from the rest of the sleepers. When he reached the other side, he heard soft moaning noises. He discovered the source of the moans underneath one of the trees.

At first, he didn't recognize them. He saw the slim nude body of a young woman leaning against the trunk of the tree. Her breasts were small, girlish. A man stood behind her. His naked buttocks clenched as he slowly moved his lower body back and forth. With every forward thrust, the girl in front of him let out a suppressed moan.

When the girl turned her head, a ray of moonlight falling through the branches briefly illuminated her face. As Wang had suspected, it was Mirna. He also recognized Mirko, the young Amaarin soldier.

Mirko pulled his penis out of Mirna. She fell to her knees and lifted up her rump. He knelt behind her, grabbed her narrow hips and pushed forward. His stiff pole disappeared between the girl's white buttocks. Arching her back, she let out a soft cry as he slid deep into her.

In the stillness of the night, Wang heard the gentle slaps as Mirko's belly slammed repeatedly into Mirna's soft buttocks.

"Faster," she whispered fiercely. "No need to be gentle."

Mirko put his hands on her shoulders, began to move with ever-increasing speed. The girl whimpered and clawed the grassy ground, gyrating her slim body beneath him.

A soft hand touched Wang's shoulder. Startled, he turned around.

"I'm ready," Tamsy whispered, tugging on his belt. He let her push down his pants. His penis jumped out, thick and hard. Without waiting to get completely naked, Wang pushed Tamsy onto her back and fell between her spreading legs. With a cry, he slid into her creamy sex-organ. She wrapped her slim legs around his torso and let her heels rest on his clenching buttocks. Her vagina engulfed his hard organ like a tight velvety glove. Waves of pleasure radiated through his whole body. Sucking on her nipples, he swallowed the intoxicating honey-sweet elixir that gushed from her breast, and he felt strength flowing into every fiber of his body.

Xandra-born did not copulate to just propagate their race. They needed to have intercourse with a True-Human to collect seeds for the Xandra, which meant they had to offer more than a True-Human female.

They offered a male ultimate pleasure. What other reason could there be for a man to seek out the daughters of the Xandra?

Wang had never before known the level of pleasure he experienced with Tamsy. She was like a drug to him. Would he ever be free of her?

He looked into her shiny green eyes and drank the beauty of her face, as she moved on top of him. She smiled, her inner muscles rippled gently the length of his hard organ, like a million tiny feathers. He couldn't hold back any longer and with a shout, he released his sperm into her. He shuddered in her arms for what seemed an eternity of bliss.

"I will take your gift to the Mother," she whispered, making him pull out.

He rolled onto his back, closed his eyes and listened to the moans and cries coming from the tree where he had observed Mirna and Mirko. He heard a rustling in the grass as someone approached. Moments later soft fingers encircled his penis and moved gently up and down. Keeping his eyes closed, he smiled, enjoying the touch of the hand. "Don't tease," he said after awhile, laughing softly. "Climb on top."

A moment of hesitation, then he sensed her straddling him. The warm, fat lips of her vagina touched the tip of his penis, parted to let him slide into hot moistness. At first, she moved slowly, but soon her buttocks slammed into his thighs as she impaled herself deeper on his hard shaft.

He kept his eyes shut and concentrated on the feel of her sheath sliding over his penis. She felt different, not quite as tight, but she was soft and wet and doused his thighs with her warm discharge. He couldn't hold it for very long this time. Ready to explode inside her, he opened his eyes to watch her face.

"Surprise," said a woman's laughing haughty voice.

"Lyra!" he exclaimed, shocked, but unable to hold back

She clamped down hard when she felt him jetting, closed her eyes and milked him fiercely until he was finished, then she relaxed on top of him and gave him a broad smile. "When I saw you lying there with that satisfier of yours sticking straight into the air I couldn't help myself. The power of those purple flowers is hard to resist, you know."

"What about Esram, your husband?" Wang stammered.

Lyra laughed, wriggled her bottom around his stiff penis. "Don't mind him, he's fast asleep. Nothing wakes him up. Besides, an old woman like me needs a young buck inside her once in awhile." She padded her slightly protruding belly. "Too bad I'm already carrying one inside me. I wouldn't mind some new blood."

"I can't get used to your morality," Wang said, embarrassed by the older woman's frankness.

Lyra lifted up a little and sank back down, her vagina contracted around his penis. She laughed when Wang moaned. "I may be a little old, but I can still give a man great pleasure, even one as young as you. Lots of experience. And I must admit--I am enjoying it immensely." She began rotating her wide hips. Wang stared at her breasts; they were large, slightly sagging, but with a firmness he didn't suspect on a woman of her age.

A shadow loomed over him. When he looked he saw Tamsy kneeling beside them. She smiled, bent and offered one of her breasts. Without thinking, he took the long nipple into his mouth and began sucking.

He possessed incredible stamina, and so did Lyra. She rode him with great enthusiasm, cried out when an orgasm racked her body. Her warm discharge ran into his pubic hair, down the insides of his thighs. He kept sucking on Tamsy's breasts while inside Lyra. She stopped moving before he could come again inside her, freed him and knelt beside him.

"That is the best one I have had, young man," she said, after catching her breath. Then she laughed softly. "I see--you are still ready to carry on. I'm sure this little girl here is quite willing to finish what I started." She settled down in the grass and watched Tamsy take her place.

Moving her buttocks with lightning speed, the Xandra-girl brought Wang to another shattering climax. This time his penis stood only half erect when Tamsy left him. Both, Lyra and Wang, watched the girl run to the pond to deliver the pouch with Wang's seeds.

"These Xandra-girls are surely beautiful." Lyra sighed. "A human woman has a hard time competing with them."

Wang agreed, but kept it to himself. He was listening to the love-sounds coming from nearby. When he looked, he saw the highlighted silhouette of a slim girl on all fours. A male crouched on top of her, his hips moved lazily back and forth. Wang could see the young man's stiff penis as it disappeared between the girl's white buttocks. Another male knelt in front of her, his penis buried inside her mouth.

Wang could hear the girl's soft moans and the grunting of the men. If Lyra was aware of what went on not far from them, she didn't betray herself. "I better get back," she said after awhile. She gave Wang a quick kiss on the cheek and whispered, "Thank you."

She got up and slipped a thin nightgown over her head, then she hurried away, back to the sleepers.

Wang decided not to judge her. Everything on this planet was alien to him, even the Humans. Looking up into the night-sky, he wondered about the location of the giant station of the Genaar at this moment. The two satellites were drifting apart, the third one appeared above the treetops.

Another two days and they should be meeting up with the shuttle at the edge of the city. In the morning, he would try to contact Lambert to get an update on Commander Beringer's condition.

Chapter Twelve

The news was not good. Lambert told him that Starmote and Reyna had taken the dying Commander to the City, with the hope that the Xandra would cure his illness. With Commander Beringer and Starmote gone, Wang became the commanding office. He could tell Lambert to come and pick him up, but decided against it. Lambert and his passengers would just have to wait until he got there with the wagon train. He told Lambert to sit tight or wait for orders from Starmote.

Spending two more days on horseback did not create much enthusiasm for Wang, but he had promised Tamsy to protect her and her sisters until they arrived at the City. He would not break that promise. Besides, he didn't really find it an unpleasant duty.

Thinking about the night, he smiled. What a night it had been! Tamsy had, of course, been no surprise--but Lyra? What a woman! What fire! Lucky Esram.

Wang felt a bit puzzled at breakfast. Lyra behaved as if nothing happened. She acted polite, but quite cool towards him. And then there was Mirna, her daughter! She could not have been oblivious the night before to Wang's and Tamsy's presence, or even her mother's.

At least two of the Amaarin soldiers had been with her sexually. It would come to no surprise to Wang to find out that all five of the young men had *fogged* her during the night.

Again, he had no intention to judge.

Only once, during breakfast, he noticed Mirna staring at him, and it seemed that she wanted to say something. But she didn't. It might have had nothing to do with the night's event, anyway.

Tamsy decided to ride one of the horses and she stayed close to Wang, as if afraid to let him get too far away from her. "Do you prefer Human women?" she asked suddenly.

Her question surprised Wang a little. He wondered what bothered her. "Why do you ask?"

Tamsy shrugged. "Just curious. The woman, Lyra, came to you last night. Did you like spilling your seed into her?"

Embarrassed by her naive frankness, Wang smiled. "Yes, I did, but your presence made it more pleasurable. By the way, I don't think we should discuss it. Lyra may not want anyone else to know."

"You mean her husband Esram?"

"Especially her husband."

Shaking her head, Tamsy said, "Human-born like to have secrets. I don't understand it."

"Some things are best kept hidden," Wang advised her.

After riding silently beside him for a while, Tamsy said, "You never answered my question."

"About my preference?" He shrugged and asked, "Would it make you happy if I told you I prefer you?"

"Yes, it would." She gave a little laugh. "I prefer you, too."

Wang found it difficult not to think of her as human. He knew that she had been grown inside a seed-pouch, never knew a mother or a father, and yet--she was not much different from any human girl he ever knew. "Why must you go the City?" he asked. "Couldn't you collect seeds for the Xandra anywhere? Seems to me the Xandra-plants are in every pond."

"I could, but this time it is different. I am in seed."

"I don't understand."

Tamsy shook her head. "You don't know much about the daughters of the Xandra, do you, Wang?"

"No, I don't, but I'm trying to learn."

"As a Xandra-born I cannot grow life inside my belly, like a human woman, but every five cycles I grow a seed-pod. If it becomes fertilized by a human male, it leaves my belly. I must deposit it into the water, where it lies until the life inside the pod gets too big and then it will burst out of its shell."

"You mean you lay an egg?" Wang asked, perplexed.

Tamsy nodded, smiled. "Yes, an egg."

"And from this egg a child is born? Incredible. What happens to this child? How big is it?"

Tamsy shrugged. "Not very big. It grows bigger inside the water. When it is about half as big as I am, it will crawl out of the water and live on land. Most of the *Water-born* don't live very long, because they are not smart enough to survive by themselves. And that is why I must go the City. My child will be raised under the protection of the Xandra. It will be smart."

"So the Xandra-born *can* have children?"

"Many, if we so wish. But we can never be mothers to them."

"I don't think I understand this whole thing. Why could you not raise your own offspring?"

"How could we? They grow in the water." She looked thoughtful and shrugged. "The desire to be a mother is not in me."

From the rear of the wagon train came the sound of female voices, singing female voices. Tamsy clapped her hands together and laughed. "I will go join my sisters, to sing and talk with them. Maybe tonight you want to put your seed into one of them."

Not human, after all, Wang thought with a stab of regret. *Human in appearance, but alien in thought and behavior.* He dug his heels into the horse's flanks and galloped to the head of the column, where Robar rode by himself. The two big hounds trotted ahead of him, their heads high, and their eyes keen and alert. They almost looked gentle, with their shiny, shaggy coats, but then Wang remembered the night back at the farm.

"A shame about your other two hounds," Wang remarked to Robar when he caught up with him.

Robar threw Wang a surprised look. "Yes, a shame, but they were just animals, and getting old. I'll breed *Ripper* and *Tooth*. By next year we'll have half a dozen pups."

"I'm glad to hear that." Wang didn't know what else to say. Robar seemed angry and irritated.

"I saw you spill your seed into Lyra, my mother, last night," Robar said, suddenly, his voice almost a growl.

Robar's fierce words took Wang by surprise. "I didn't search her out," he defended himself, his face hot.

"I know you are not to blame. She is like that. Just like Mirna, my sister. Esram is not father to all of us, you know. The child Lyra is carrying, it is not his."

"How do you know?"

"Because it is mine." Robar forced the words from his lips.

"Yours? You mean you had sex with your own mother?" Wang said, shocked and disbelieving. "Why are you telling me this?"

"To warn you. The Xandra is a great seductress and you must forever be on guard against her influences. Why did you not resist Lyra last night?"

Wang shook his head. "I had my eyes closed when she came to me. When I realized who she was, it was too late."

"I watched you, you didn't protest too much."

"It never entered my mind. There was Tamsy; there was the strong scent of those purple flowers in the air. I couldn't help myself."

Robar cursed under his breath and stared at Wang. "Once you're under the Great Mother's spell you cannot resist. You don't care into whose belly you put your spear, be it your mother or your sister."

Wang thought of Mirna, wild, young Mirna. She didn't need the Mother's help to seduce anyone. In his mind's eye, he saw her nubile white body writhing under one of the Amaarin soldiers. Robar's image replaced that of the soldier's and understanding dawned in Wang. "Is there no woman in your life?" he asked.

Robar laughed. "Once we get to the City there will many."

"Human or Xandra-born?"

"What does it matter? Even the human women will only collect seeds for the Great Mother, none for themselves." His eyes rested on Wang. "You've never taken part in the harvest celebration?"

"As you know, I am a stranger here. All this is new to me. I will heed your warning and guard myself."

"Where do you come from?"

Wang smiled to himself. It wasn't only the Xandra he had to guard himself against. "Far from here," he said. "Very far away."

"You traveled in that flying disk?"

Nodding, Wang said, "Yes, I did."

"Aran told me of that masked woman who claimed to be a goddess. Apparently, she caught the bullets with her hands and threw bolts of lightning that killed. Was she flesh and blood, or just an illusion of the mind? The Xandra can make you believe things are real, when they are not." Robar's tone of voice changed. He didn't behave as belligerent as before.

Chang smiled. "She was real. You know her. Her name is Starmote. She is one of my companions." He didn't think a little bit of truth would do any harm. "She is no goddess, but neither is she human. I don't know much about her kind."

"How so?" Robar sounded perplexed. "You say she is one of your companions."

"She is and she isn't." Wang had no intentions to give away more information. "Maybe some day I'll explain, but right now I am not allowed. Wait until we get to the City."

"You are as evasive and mysterious as the *Naar*," Robar complained.

"Who are they?"

Robar grinned. "If you don't know about them I won't be the one to tell you. You don't really want to know."

95

The harsh barking of the hounds made Robar reach for his rifle, which he had slung across his shoulders. A group of riders came out of a small grove of trees.

While talking with Tamsy and Robar, Wang paid little attention to the surrounding landscape. They left the forest some time ago and the land gradually sloped downward. The trees became shorter and less numerous. He could hear the river somewhere to his left, hidden behind tall shrubbery. At the far horizon to his right, a mountain ridge cut into the reddening sky and Wang realized that night wasn't far away.

He watched the riders come closer, counted a dozen men in uniforms. His hand went to his sidearm.

"Relax," Robar told him, "those are the Xandra's soldiers. We have nothing to fear."

The soldiers spread out, blocked the road a short distance away. One of them came closer. "I am Captain Rondar," he said, holding his rifle casually in his hands. His eyes rested on Wang while he spoke.

"I am Robar of the Refinger-Family. We are farmers, on our way to the City to take part in the harvest festival."

"And you?" The captain's eyes were still on Wang.

"My name is Darrin of the Wang-Family. I am a friend of the Refinger-Family." Wang kept his hand away from his weapon. No need to provoke anyone.

"You are a soldier," the captain stated. "Your uniform is not familiar, but if this farmer vouches for you then I have no quarrel with you." His gaze traveled the length of the wagon train; he stiffened when he saw the Amaarin soldiers. "Are they also with you?" he asked Robar.

Robar nodded. "They asked to accompany us to the City. Apparently, they are fugitives from their own country."

"Fugitives? Interesting. I think I will have a word with them."

Wang had been studying the captain and the others. They were all big men, dressed in tight-fitting black uniforms, which left their arms bare. They bristled with weapons. Knifes, swords, and rifles. A couple of them carried crossbows.

Something about them didn't look right, and Wang guessed what it was.

None were human, their faces and bodies just too perfect.

The captain and two of his men rode to the back of the wagon train. After talking briefly to the Amaarins, the Xandra-soldiers came back. "Make sure they stay out of trouble," he told Robar, then he and his men turned their horses and rode back toward the grove of trees.

"I was under the impression that all Xandra-born believe in non-violence," Wang said to Robar.

"Not these. They were specially bred to defend the Great Mother and the City. You don't want to anger them." Robar looked toward the setting sun. "We better move on, it will be dark soon, and we should not be in the open after dark."

"Do you have a destination in mind?"

"There is a small town close by. We will stay there tonight."

Even though they were descending from higher ground, the land was not even. The road began to lead slightly uphill, and Wang noticed that the horses were straining against their yokes. When Wang crested the hill, he saw houses in the distance ahead. Looking down, he also saw the slow moving water of the river, quite wide at this point. Spotting a few boats in the water, he remarked on it. Robar explained that the people in this town were mostly fishermen. An abundance of different fish lived in the river and in the big lake, on whose shores the City had been built.

"You will see many boats from now on," Robar said. "You may be surprised when you see the big ships in the lake. There is another, smaller city on the other side of the lake. Both cities trade with each other."

They reached the town shortly after dark and lit torches to see where they were going. Reaching a large fenced-in space on the outskirts of the town reserved for the wagons and animals of travelers, they drove the wagons inside and began to set up camp.

"I'm not working tonight," announced Lyra. "There is a nice, comfortable eatery in this town where they serve good food."

"Mostly fish," Robar said to Wang. "But the food is very tasty, if you like fish."

Wang noticed a couple of buildings nearby. Light fell from the small windows. The door opened on one of the houses and a couple of men came out and walked toward the corral.

Both men carried rifles.

Esram greeted them at the gate and talked to them for a while. After the two men left, Esram came back. "That was Old Ramil and his nephew. They've agreed to rub down our horses and water them, too. I promised him a sack of grain."

Once they were set up, the whole family, Wang, and the Amaarin soldiers rode into town. The Xandra-girls decided to stay in the compound, except for Tamsy. She joined Wang on his horse. Sitting behind him, she put her arms around his chest and pressed herself against his back. "I'm not letting you out of my sight, Wang," she whispered into his ear.

Wang chuckled, enjoying the feel of her soft breasts against his body. They rode the dirt road in silence. The road lay in almost complete darkness, the only illumination coming from the flickering lights that fell through the windows of the houses lining the road.

The marketplace of the town bustled with people. Torches and lanterns lit up the various stalls, where the vendors offered their wares. A strong odor of smoked and frying fish hung in the air.

"For a small town this place is quite alive," Wang remarked.

"Many of these people are travelers on their way to the harvest celebration," Robar explained. "It is not always like this."

"Where do we eat?" permeated

"Over there."

The majority of the party headed for an eating establishment in one of the side streets. The Amaarin soldiers had other plans. After tying their horses to designated poles, they decided to try the food of one of the vendors. "We may not be welcome in that place," Mirko, the speaker of the group, explained to Mirna when she asked him why he didn't want do join her.

Robar growled something under his breath and pulled Mirna with him. "You've been neglecting your son," he scolded her. "He needs his mother's breast once in awhile. He can't just live off a Xandra-born's nectar."

The Xandra-girl, who fed little Dorn most of the time lately, had stayed behind with the other girls. For a change, Mirna carried her child with her.

"He's doing fine," Mirna said. "And I do need some time away from him."

"Well, then be careful who you spread your legs for," Robar said, his voice low. "You're not ready for another child."

Mirna shook away his hand, walked angrily through the open door into the inn. The place appeared quite full, but they managed to find a couple of unoccupied tables. Wang and Tamsy sat at the same table as Esram and Lyra.

A sudden thought entered Wang's mind. It occurred to him that he probably had to pay for what he was about to order. Things like that are easily forgotten when you are a soldier. The company provided for all the basic needs, like food, clothing, and lodging. "I have no money," he said to Esram.

The old man waved a hand. "Don't worry about that, I'll look after it." He smiled. "After all, without you and your friends we probably wouldn't be sitting here tonight."

The food they ate tasted different from the food Wang was accustomed to, but he found it pleasing to the palate. The flesh of the fish was white and odorless, heavily spiced, and the vegetables, a kind of tuber, were quite good. He didn't care much for the wine, he found it too warm and a bit strong. Since he had never been a heavy drinker of alcoholic beverages, he only drank a small amount.

Esram, on the other hand, downed a few cups and seemed to be in high spirits toward the end of the meal.

Wang looked around the room. Most of the patrons were farmers with their families or hired hands. A couple of older men came over to Esram and Lyra's table, to talk and to share a cup of wine with them. Even Lyra drank more than she should have. Her laughter rang through the room.

Tamsy seemed quite subdued. Wang noticed her looking toward a table hidden in a darker corner. There were only two people at that table. He couldn't tell if they were men or women, because their bodies were covered with gray, loose robes, their faces hidden inside deep hoods.

"Is there a problem, Tamsy?" Wang asked the girl when she edged closer to him.

Her gaze flicked toward the table with the robed people. "Naar," she said.

"Naar?" Wang repeated. "Robar mentioned them. Are you talking about those two hooded ones over there?"

She nodded; her green eyes seemed even larger than usual. He could tell that she was scared.

"They're not bothering us," he said, not understanding her fear.

"But they will. I've seen them looking at me." She shuddered, clasped his arm.

"You are a beautiful girl." Wang smiled. "Men will look at you."

"You promised to protect me, Wang," she said. "Will you?"

"Of course, I will. Come, you've barely touched your food."

Wang kept watching the two gray-robed ones, his curiosity aroused. *You don't really want to know*, Robar had said. But now he did. They rose from their seats and walked toward the exit. Their path took them past Wang's table, where they stopped for a quick moment. One of them bowed toward Wang, then they both moved on.

Beside him, Tamsy stiffened, visibly shaken by the incident. "I'm afraid," she whispered.

"They didn't even pay any attention to you," Wang said. "I think you are imagining things." He grinned. "Too bad I didn't get a good look at their faces. They may have been a couple of good looking women." He put an arm around Tamsy's shoulders and held her for moment when he felt her trembling. "Don't worry; I won't let anyone harm you."

After eating, the rest of the group decided to do some shopping at the market.

"I want to get back to my sisters," Tamsy told Wang. He nodded. "I have no money for shopping, anyway," he said, "and frankly, I'm quite tired and my backside is sore."

Wang untied the horse. Before he mounted the animal, he helped Tamsy onto its broad back.

The sky seemed to brighten, Wang could see one of the moons rise above the far mountains. They rode a short distance, when a group of riders suddenly barred the road.

They were dressed in gray robes.

"We want the Xandra-born," one of them said.

"She is not mine to give," Wang said, "but even if she were, the answer would be no."

"Then we take her!"

One of the gray riders put something to his lips. Wang felt a sharp stinging pain in his neck. He began slipping off his horse, tried to hold on with his hands, but all strength had left his fingers.

He didn't remember falling to the ground.

Chapter Thirteen

Waking up slowly, Beringer became aware of the soft bed he lay in. Opening his eyes, he saw bright moonlight streaming through an opening in the wall. A gentle warm breeze blew through the opening, caressing his naked skin. He inhaled the familiar intoxicating fragrance that clung to the air. When he heard the whisper of bare feet on stone, he turned his head to look at the woman who came through a curtain that covered the entrance to his room.

"I presume you are feeling well, Commander," she said.

"Starmote?" Beringer sat up and looked into her alien black eyes.

She smiled and sat down at the edge of the bed. The thin gown she wore molded itself against her breasts. Through the almost transparent material he could see the delicate markings on her skin.

"Why are you dressed like that?" he asked.

She laughed. "Would you rather see me naked?"

"You know I would, but this is just as good," he grinned, became serious. "What happened?"

She put a hand on his arm. It felt smooth against his skin, smooth and warm, and exiting.

"You were quite sick," she said. "The Shadow-Angel drank much of your blood and injected you with a poisonous substance. But don't blame the poor creature, it is not her fault."

"Where are we?" Beringer looked at the softly swaying branches of tall trees outside of his window. He could see the surface of a large pond, people moved around in the grass covering the shore.

"You are in the City of the Great Mother," Starmote said. She stood up, lifted the gown over her head and removed it. Naked, she stood in front of him.

Beringer stared at her perfect body, her large, solid breasts, the curve of her hip, her long, slender legs. "What are you doing?" he asked.

Smiling, she lay down beside him, rolled onto her side and let her fingers trail down his chest. When she reached his groin, her fingers curled around his penis and squeezed it gently. His penis hardened and grew in her hand.

"It still works," she laughed and moved on top of him, rubbing her genitals over his hardness. He could feel her soft moist cleft on his swollen head. Sitting up, she straddled him. When he looked, he saw that her mons pubis was thick and without a trace of hair. She raised her body; his stiff shaft snapped between her opening thighs. With a cry of pleasure, he slid into incredible softness.

Her black alien eyes stared into his as her hips gyrated with slow motion in his lap. "Isn't that what you wanted all along?" she whispered.

He nodded, dumbfounded, and clenched his jaw in an effort to keep from exploding inside her tight sheath.

Not yet... not yet... he told himself. *I've waited so long for her and I don't want it to be over so soon.*

As if sensing what went through his mind, she smiled gently and said, "Go ahead. I promise you'll be able to go on."

With an exultant roar he let go and climaxed with tremendous force. She milked him until he came down from his incredible high, tired but still stiff.

She bent down and kissed him. Sweet nectar dribbled from her mouth into his and ran down his throat. He swallowed, feeling renewed vigor. Putting his arms around her, he rolled her onto her back and moved between her widespread legs. She sucked him deep into her, pushed against him as he took her with forceful strokes.

When he suckled on her breasts, he drank the sweet liquid that flowed from them. Levels of pleasure he had not experienced before radiated through his whole body. He filled her vessel again and again, roared with a voice gone hoarse, not caring if anyone heard. When he couldn't go on any longer, he lay panting beside her, his body clammy with perspiration.

"I am totally exhausted," he said, trying to catch his breath. "You didn't even break into a sweat."

She laughed throatily, sat up. "I never tire."

He cupped her breast, squeezed it gently. "You taste good," he said.

She slipped from the bed, stood looking down at him.

Bolting upright, he stared at her long, flaming red hair, looked into her green eyes. "You are not Starmote," he said slowly, as the truth dawned on him.

Laughing, she shook her hair. "I am The Xandra," she said.

"I could have sworn you were Starmote. How did you... how is it possible...?"

"When your Genaar companion entered my temple, I scanned her down to her last molecule. I know everything about her--and you." Her outlines shimmered, changed. He saw Reyna looking at him out of large green eyes. "And I know everything about this daughter of mine," the Xandra said in Reyna's voice.

She changed back, became the human looking woman with the flaming red hair. Beringer kept staring at her, captivated by her almost unearthly beauty.

"You humans are obsessed with the concept of beauty," the Xandra said. "It is one of your weaknesses." Her breasts heaved as she sighed deeply. "When I am in this form I also love perfection and beauty. I am, in fact, human."

"Are you real, or just an illusion?" Beringer asked.

She chuckled. "I am real. You were joined with me. Did that not feel real?"

He shook his head. "You seem to read my thoughts. As far as I know you could have manipulated my mind, made me believe I had sex with you."

Smiling, she laid a hand on his cheek. It felt warm, real. "This is reality, Commander Les Beringer. This body is real, and you and I had sexual intercourse. Your orgasm was real. I received your seeds into my body and I will use them to create new life. I am a Goddess, all powerful, and I have created most of the creatures that live on this planet."

"So why put on this charade? What need do you have to copulate with a human mortal man?"

"Even though I have great powers, I am not omnipotent. I cannot create life from nothing; I need the living sperms of a male." She smiled. "I could extract it from you without giving you pleasure, but that would be wasteful. Therefore, I create a beautiful woman. I give her all the desires a human woman has. I give her the ability to experience pleasure. What she experiences, I experience. Can you imagine the pure pleasure of having sex with thousands of partners at the same time?"

"I can't say that I do," Beringer murmured.

"I could share the experience with you."

"No, thank you. I won't let you mess with my mind."

"What makes you so sure I haven't done so already?" she asked mockingly. "Tell me, Beringer, why are you here?"

Beringer smiled thinly. "I thought you knew me intimately. Then you must know the answer to that question."

She laughed without malice. "The human mind is a complex thing. I can see into your thoughts, but much is hidden from my probing. I have no desire to go into the recesses of your mind and search for the information I seek. Even though it would be an easy thing to do."

"Why don't you then?"

"My probing would not leave you untouched." She smiled. "You want to find out what happened on the planet while you slept for a thousand years?"

When he looked surprised, she laughed. "There are many ways to extract information. You have to learn to control your thoughts, Commander."

"I've never had to deal with a telepath before." Beringer couldn't keep his eyes off her. Her beauty seemed almost intimidating.

She read his thoughts and laughed gaily. "Would it surprise you if I told you I enjoy being admired?" she asked.

"It would," he said. "You are a goddess."

"Even a goddess has desires," she said and put her hand on his erection.

He groaned, let her push him back onto the bed and straddle him. Watching his erect penis enter her sex-organ, he noticed that her mons was covered with a carpet of fine golden-red hair.

Reading his thoughts, she smiled down at him. "Making love to me is always exciting," she whispered. "I can be any woman you want me to be."

Suddenly Starmote writhed above him. The markings on her skin faded, she became Reyna. Her skin darkened, became black. From her shoulders sprouted large wings.

Beringer stiffened and whispered hoarsely, "Naomi!"

She displayed needle-thin fangs. "I am not she," she said in Naomi's voice, "just her image. I know you craved her body."

She changed again. Mirna's slim body undulated in his lap. Her adolescent breasts were small, underdeveloped. They grew as it occurred to him they should be larger. Even though young, she was already a mother, a woman.

Her vagina tightened around his penis. It proved too much. With a deep moan, he erupted, turned on tremendously by the thought of having sex with such a young woman, secure in the knowledge that it really wasn't her.

The image of Mirna laughed, her girlish hips a blur in his lap, and her narrow cleft clamped like a soft vice around his engorged organ. "I know your secret desires," she said, her vagina a living, moving thing between her slim thighs.

When he neared another climax, she bent close to him and whispered into his ear, "In the throes of your orgasm your thoughts are wide open to my probing."

He didn't care, grabbed her slim hips and lunged upward to fill her again with his discharge.

She entered his mind, stimulated his pleasure center. The level of pleasure became too high. He blacked out.

* * * *

When Beringer regained his senses, he found himself alone. It was daylight. Through a large open window, he saw the fruit-laden branches of a tall tree. Sitting up, he noticed that soft blankets covered the bed he lay in. They were wrinkled, bundled together in an untidy heap. Looking down at himself, he noticed that he was naked.

Fragments of what seemed like a vivid dream clung to his consciousness, but he knew it had not been a dream.

Beside the bed lay a pile of clothing, neatly stacked together. He recognized them as his. Sliding his feet off the bed, he stood up and stretched. He should be tired, exhausted, but he felt refreshed and rested.

Picking up his clothes, he put them on, feeling even better after getting dressed.

He walked over to the window and looked out. He saw a small lake, surrounded by tall trees, and people walking on graveled paths that led through large beds of blooming flowers.

"Beautiful, isn't it?" said a male voice from behind him.

A familiar male voice.

Surprised, he turned around and stared at the man standing in the room. "Captain Cunningham?" His voice sounded hollow in his own ears. A cold shiver ran down his spine.

The man stood there, smiling. He wore a shiny, brand-new uniform. Holding out a hand, he walked toward Beringer. "Les," he said, "How have you been? It's been awhile, old friend."

Beringer didn't move. "You are not Jeremy Cunningham. You can't be. He's dead a thousand years."

"Has it been that long? How time flies." The man chuckled.

"It hasn't been that long for me. Only three weeks since I saw the Captain alive," Beringer said.

"That's right, you were frozen. Courtesy of our new found allies, the Genaar. How's my old friend Starfinder?"

Beringer put his hand to his temple and closed his eyes for a moment. This man acted and talked just like Captain Cunningham. It would be easy to shake his hand, clap him on the shoulder. Opening his eyes, he said, "Stop it! You are not the Captain. Why don't you change back into a woman? I liked you better that way."

"Sorry, can't oblige you. I'm stuck with this body." Cunningham smiled. "I guess some explanations are in order. You are correct, I am not the original Jeremy Cunningham, but I have all his memories, well…not all of them, only up to the last time he…I came down to the planet. The Cunningham you remember wasn't the original, either. I guess you know that."

"I had my suspicions." Beringer studied the man in the captain's uniform. "So, what are you then?" he asked.

"A duplicate, of course. You might say I am a clone. If the Xandra hadn't told me, I wouldn't know. As far as I'm concerned, I am Captain Jeremy Cunningham." He sighed. "The Xandra told me what happened a thousand years ago. What I mean…she put the knowledge into my memories. I also know much of what happened since then."

"Why are you here?"

"Call me Jeremy. After all, we were good friends, and you used to call me by my first name." He sat down at the edge of the bed and looked up at Beringer. "I missed you, my friend. For you it may be only three weeks since you saw me last, for me it's been over twenty years."

"I've read your journals," Beringer said slowly.

"Then you know what happened? Things began to fall apart at the station. How did I die? Did I still have some dignity left?"

"You took your own life. And yes, you died with dignity."

"I'm glad to hear that." Cunningham chuckled, opened and closed his hands. "I am alive again and I feel great. I should have joined the settlers on the planet, instead of staying on the station. I could have saved myself a lot of grief. Mind you, I was not unhappy. The Xandra gave me back my wife."

"It wasn't really your wife, Jeremy, only a simulacrum. Just like you are now," Beringer said bitterly.

"You're wrong, Les. I am Jeremy Cunningham. This body may be artificially grown, but all my memories are intact."

"They're imprints, that's all. You're not human. You have no soul."

"No soul? Does Reyna have a soul?"

"I don't know. How can you even know about her?"

"As I told you, the Xandra put a lot of information into my head. I may have been dead for a thousand years, but I am pretty much up to date." He stood up, walked over to the open window, looked out at the lake. "We called this planet *Nu-Eden*. Then we discovered a serpent. Just like in the original Eden."

"If you believe that story," Beringer murmured beside him.

Cunningham glanced at Beringer. "Are you a religious man, Les?" he asked.

Beringer shook his head. "Not particularly. I believe what I see."

"And yet you believe that man has a soul. I find that interesting. I was a religious man," Cunningham paused, smiled. "I *am* a religious man, and I believe in a higher power. I believe in good and evil." He turned toward Beringer. "The Xandra is not evil. She is not the serpent in the Garden of Eden. Man is!"

"What is the Xandra, Jeremy?"

"She is a goddess."

Beringer snorted. "Come on. Tell that to old women and little children."

"Alright." Cunningham grabbed Beringer's arm. "Come, let us go for a walk."

They stepped through the window opening, onto a graveled path.

"What is this place?" Beringer asked.

"This is the birthplace of the Xandra, the Great Mother. She lives underneath the temple, in a huge cavern. You were there, but I guess you don't remember anything." Cunnigham stopped beside a bench under a tree with wide spreading branches. "Let's sit down, stay out of the sun."

"The sun bothers you?"

"No more than you. This body is not very different form my old one, except that it is healthier, younger."

"You were telling me about the Xandra." Beringer sat down beside Cunningham.

"Right, I was. The Xandra is old, very old. For millennia, she existed only in a semi-sentient state, half plant, half something else. She lived in symbiosis with the only other sentient beings, the tree-elves. Their intelligence is lower than that of a monkey; at least it was then. There are only male tree-elves, no females. The Xandra-plant is carnivorous; it feeds on living flesh. One might say the tree-elves were on the lower end of the Xandra's food chain. By exuding pheromones she would attract them, get them sexually aroused. They would climb onto the Xandra-plant, have sexual intercourse with the plant and spill their seeds into a rudimentary sex-organ, which the plant created. After intercourse the plant would feed." The Captain chuckled. "It is not uncommon. There were similar things on Earth. The *Praying Mantis*, or the *Black Widow* spider, for instance."

Beringer smiled. "I can think of worse ways to go, I guess. So what happened to the seeds the plant collected?"

"They grew inside special seed-pouches and developed into tree-elves. And the cycle began again."

"The Xandra-born are still created that way."

"Yes, except in the beginning there were only tree-elves. Then an extraordinary thing happened. Visitors from another world landed. You can guess--the Genaar. Two thousand years ago. For the first time the Xandra encountered an intelligence greater than hers. She wasn't aware of the visitors until she consumed one of the Genaar females. From the mind of this female she learned of the Genaar. When she snared a Genaar male by assuming the form of a Genaar female her primitive intelligence received a boost from the encounter. the Xandra began to evolve, became more intelligent. You may not know this, but the Genaar do not bear young the way humans do. They are egg layers, but the females do breastfeed their hatched young," Cunningham grinned. "That's why they have breasts, in case you wondered."

"I haven't." Beringer smiled. "But the information is interesting."

"Anyway, the Xandra-plant learned about sex and pleasure. She figured out a way to create more of these new beings. She introduced the females to seed-pouches. By putting the gelatin-like films into her vagina, a female could increase her own pleasure and that of her male partner.

Unfortunately, the Xandra, in her ignorance, made a mistake. She consumed all the Genaar males and females on the planet and cloned them again from her own body. The males she created were sterile. She began using the tree-elves as sperm donors, but only females were born. For a thousand years, the Xandra lay dormant. Then the humans came."

"And the Great Mother made the same mistake all over. She ate them all," Beringer said dryly.

"Not all, only the first wave of settlers. She realized that she needed the human males in their original form. As you've noticed, there are quiet a number of True-Humans on this planet now."

"I know, and not all of them are worshipping the Great Goddess, either." Beringer looked at Cunningham, willing to accept him, for now. "Tell me, what is the situation on Nu-Eden? Or are you not allowed to talk about it?"

Cunningham laughed. "Still the skeptic. I am not bound to the Xandra. There is nothing she forbade me to tell you. In fact, regard me as the liaison's officer between you and the Xandra. I'll tell you what I know."

"You mean you'll tell me what the Xandra programmed you to say."

Cunningham heaved a sigh. "Whatever you want to believe. I realize, I only know what she put into my memory, but deep down I know that it is the truth. I can still reason, Les. I am not a puppet of the Xandra. I am Jeremy Cunningham, a free man."

"Well…then tell me about Nu-Eden."

"Much has changed since the first colonists landed. Humans have had a great impact on the way things developed. Humans were also instrumental in the evolution of the Xandra."

"Not the Genaar?" Beringer asked.

"The arrival of the Genaar stimulated the intellect of the Xandra, but the Humans brought her excitement, dreams, and the concept of conflict."

"I'm sure the Genaar have had their share of conflict." Beringer said.

"Oh, they did." Cunningham nodded. But the Xandra never absorbed the diversity of Genaar who would have given her the knowledge and experience the humans brought with them. The first Genaar colonists were scientists, farmers and laborers. The females were all courtesans; their job was to keep the workforce happy."

"Fascinating!" Beringer commented. "Starfinder never mentioned courtesans."

The Captain chuckled. "There was a lot our friend Starfinder didn't mention."

Both men looked up when they heard the footsteps of someone approaching. With surprise Beringer looked at the naked young girl stopping in front of them. She appeared to be no older than about ten

Standard years. She was not human. She had the large, purple eyes of a Genaar.

"The Mother would like to see you," the girl said to Cunningham.

The Captain nodded. "We'll be there."

The little girl smiled, turned and rushed to join a group of children who came streaming out of a door. Beringer stared after her.

"She's one of the Water-born," Cunningham said.

"I thought the Xandra-born couldn't reproduce?" Beringer asked.

"They can, but not like humans. Come, let's go and see what the Xandra wants."

Cunningham led the Commander to a door that allowed them entrance into the temple. They walked down a narrow corridor, and then through a door into a small room. Two women sat facing each other on thick pillows on the floor. Beringer recognized the woman who called herself The Xandra. Her red luxurious hair cascaded down her shoulders and her front, like a veil, partially covering her nude body underneath.

The other woman was Starmote. She wore her camouflage outfit. Both women looked up when the men entered. "Commander," Starmote said and smiled. "You look healthy. I trust you are feeling better."

Chapter Fourteen

"What in the name of Donar are you doing here?" Viran asked.

The girl folded her wings behind her and smiled. "Aren't you going to invite me in, Viran?"

"If its coupling with me you are looking for I'm afraid it will have to wait till morning. I am too exhausted." Viran stepped aside to let her in. Tegron came out of his room to see what was going on. He grinned when he saw the winged girl.

"This is Angela," Viran said.

Tegron looked her over. "You look different," he said. "You are bigger and taller than your sisters. What use do you have for clothing?"

Angela laughed; her blue eyes sparkled in the flickering light of the oil lamps. "To cover up what a male seeks in a woman."

"Your kind doesn't have what a male seeks," Tegron growled.

"*She* does," Viran commented dryly. "And believe me--she knows how to use it."

Angela's pearly laughter filled the room. "And Viran should know," she said.

"How did you find me?" Viran asked her.

She came closer, brushed his lips with hers. "I always know where you are." He felt a strange pulling inside his mind. *You and I are linked, my brother*. Her voice sounded like a ghostly echo in his head. She hadn't moved her lips.

He looked at her sharply, but she just smiled. Her hand moved between them to touch his penis. When he inhaled deeply, she said, "Don't worry, I can wait until morning." She stepped back, gave Tegron a studying glance. "You look like a healthy specimen of a man. All the necessary equipment, too, I see. Does it work?"

"You want to find out?" Tegron asked, a grin splitting his handsome features.

Viran just shook his head. He felt a bond between him and Angela, but her behavior began to irritate him. He missed that sweet little winged girl who had bewitched him with her innocence and tenderness. Now she reminded him of the girls back on the island, except that she was more beautiful.

"I'm going to bed," he said. "You two do what you want."

Angela sensed his irritation. She touched his shoulder; her smile gentle and soft. "I'll sleep with you, if you don't mind," she said.

He shrugged and walked into one of the bedrooms, there he stretched out on the bed. Angela followed him, removed her armor and lay down beside him. Lying on her belly, she spread her wings slightly, one of them covering Viran like a blanket of soft feathers.

He didn't sleep well. Strange and disturbing dreams plagued him most of the night. Waking up, he found Angela's warm and naked body tightly curled up against him. She had thrown her arm across his chest in a protective gesture, as if to prevent him from leaving her.

Something had aroused him from his sleep and he strained his ears to listen to the noises outside. Through the small window fell the reddish light of *Hope,* the smaller moon, who appeared when the two Wanderers, Rah and Roh, were on their journey home. The forest was never really silent. The eerie laughter of a *Redthroat* sent a slight shiver down Viran's back, silently hoping he'd never cross paths with the long-legged night runner. Viran's keen hearing detected another sound. The drumming of hoofs on trampled earth. Slipping out from under Angela's arm and off the bed, he padded silently toward the door, opened it and stepped into the kitchen. Walking up to the window, he peered through the murky glass. His vision wasn't clear, but he could see the riders in the yard, at least a dozen hooded figures on horseback. Even though he couldn't see them clearly, he knew what they were. *Naar.*

The Naar were the mysterious people who lived somewhere to the south, across the ocean. They kept to themselves, appeared and disappeared at random, to trade or to raid. What they looked like under their hooded robes nobody on the island knew. They were fierce warriors and their preferred weapon a long tube through which they blew poisoned darts. Viran had never met them. Most of his information came from Old Grisgaar. There were rumors that the Naar were neither human nor Xandra-born, but those were just rumors.

In the dark, he put on his clothing, and then he searched for his war-hammer. When he held it in his hand, confidence surged through him. He remembered suddenly what Old Grisgaar had told him…they had excellent night-vision. One of the oil lamps stood on the table and he went to light it with the spark-sticks that lay beside the lamp.

Hearing heavy footsteps on the veranda, he stood waiting for them, his war-hammer ready in his hands. The handle on the door moved, then the door swung open. Viran stared at the hooded figure that appeared in the doorway, but made no aggressive moves.

"Are you the farmer who lives here?" asked the intruder. He spoke with a strange, guttural accent.

Viran decided to tell the truth. "I am a guest in this place. The house was empty when we came here."

"There are more of you?"

"I have two companions," Viran said, his fingers gripping the handle of his hammer tightly.

"We do not seek conflict," said the hooded stranger. "You can put down your weapon."

"If you need shelter, you are welcome here," Viran said.

The Naar chuckled. "We prefer to sleep in our own shelters. The stench in these places is nauseating to us."

"I prefer to sleep under the stars myself," Viran said, "but it is safer in here. Too many dangers lurk in the forest."

"We are not afraid of those dangers." The Naar didn't hide his contempt.

"Neither are we," said a rumbling voice behind Viran. Tegron stepped out of his room, still naked.

"Your companion knows no shame," the Naar said to Viran. "Tell him that I am offended by his unclothed body."

Tegron laughed deep in his throat. "I am offended by those ugly robes you wear," he growled. "Perhaps you are ashamed of your body. I am not ashamed of mine."

The Naar hissed inside his hood. "You obviously know nothing about us."

"You are wrong, Naar, I know a lot about your kind." Tegron made a sign with his fingers, and then said something in a language Viran didn't understand.

"Where did you learn?" the Naar asked.

"A long time ago, as a slave on one of your ships!" Tegron spoke with suppressed anger.

When the Naar moved, Viran caught the reflection from the oil lamp's flame in the shadow of the hood. "You may get a chance to repeat that experience," the Naar said darkly.

"I won't be taken so easily this time," Tegron growled a warning.

The Naar chuckled. "You are naked and unarmed."

"I am not," Angela's voice came from the open door of the bedroom. She stood, dressed in her armor, a naked sword in her right hand.

"Your third companion, I assume," said the Naar, "an Angel with a sword."

"I am Angela. We are messengers of the Great Mother. Do not provoke us!"

"A threat?" The Naar laughed. "Is the Xandra not *The Mother of Light*? I thought she did not practice violence." He took a step into the room and seemed to study Angela. "Are you not supposed to be a gentle creature whose only purpose is to flitter among the trees? Why do you cover your body? There is nothing to hide."

Behind him appeared two more hooded figures. They carried thin tubes in their hands. "I am curious," the Naar leader said. "Take off your armor. I want to see what is hidden underneath."

Angela laughed and pointed her sword at him. "You take off your robe first and then I'll decide if it is worth my while to get undressed."

"Enough of this nonsense!" Viran growled. With a swift movement, he stepped beside the Naar leader, spun him around and held him like a shield in front of him. "Tell your people to go outside; they have not been invited in. Then we'll discuss the situation."

"You hurt me and you'll be dead!" warned the Naar and gave a command in his native tongue. His two companions had pushed their tubes into their hoods, but they obeyed and walked backward out of the door. Viran didn't hear their footsteps; he knew they were waiting just outside the door.

Tegron moved toward the door, closed it and laid a thick iron bar across it. "We'll be safe for awhile," he said.

Viran let go of the Naar who stepped away from him, rubbing his neck underneath his robe. "You are very strong, Islander," he said, "and fast."

"How do you know where I come from?" Viran demanded.

"The way you dress. Your weapon. Only a worshipper of the *God of Thunder* carries such a weapon."

"It seems that you know more about me than I about you."

"To know your enemy and your friends is very important to one's survival. But you and I are not enemies. I meant no harm when I asked the Angel to disrobe. I was merely curious, it is our nature."

Tegron chuckled. "It is also in your nature to be discourteous. It wouldn't hurt you to be a little more humble."

The Naar bowed toward the big man. "Our ways have insured the survival of my people. We are what we are. I apologize." He turned toward Angela. "Why are you covering your body?"

Despite the situation, Viran couldn't help but grin. "Why don't you go into the bedroom with her and find out," he suggested.

"No need." The Naar addressed Angela again. "Are you a new breed of Angel? Can you propagate?"

"I am unique. Can I have offspring? I don't know. I can join with a male, if that's what you're interested in."

"I am very much intrigued."

"Why do you want to know?" Viran asked.

"He is a collector," Tegron said.

"A collector of what?"

"New blood," answered the Naar.

"They kidnap Xandra-born females and males." Tegron explained.

"For what purpose?"

"The males to entertain their women, and the females for breeding."

Viran shook his head, not understanding. "Xandra-born don't breed. They only collect seeds for the Mother," he said.

"You are only partially correct," said the Naar. "They don't breed among themselves; but we can mate with the daughters of the Great Mother, successfully." His hand moved toward his face, which was hidden deep inside his hood. Too late Viran saw the thin tube. He also saw that it wasn't aimed at him. He heard the explosive sound of sudden expelled air, and then the falling of a heavy body.

Cursing loudly, he lifted his war-hammer, when suddenly a voice said, "Don't, Viran, no violence. Go with them peacefully." He realized it came from inside his head. The voice of the Xandra and it carried a sense of urgency.

"You are my sword-arm, Viran," the Xandra said, "but also my eyes. I must know more about the Naar."

Viran lowered his weapon. Behind him, he heard another body fall...Angela. He saw the Naar push a small object into one end of the thin tube, saw him lift it again to his mouth. "Why are you attacking us?" he asked.

"Your companion told you what we do," the Naar said.

"We would accompany you freely," Viran told him.

"I prefer this way."

Viran felt a sharp sting in his shoulder, then his awareness slipped away.

Chapter Fifteen

Wang remembered falling off his horse. He lay for moment with his eyes closed, listened to the sounds around him. The alien translator behind his ear amplified even quiet whispering.

"He doesn't look like a farmer," one male voice said.

"The weapon we took from him is definitely more advanced than anything we've ever seen," another answered.

"He must be a mercenary traveling with the farmers," said the first voice again.

Wang opened his eyes and looked around. He found himself lying on a mat inside a large tent-like structure. Two of the robed ones stood not far from him. When Wang lifted his head, he saw another one reclining on a pile of blankets.

"The prisoner is awake," said a female voice. It came from the robed figure on the blankets.

The other two stopped their discussion; one came toward Wang, bent over him. In the dim light Wang saw only a shadowy face inside the gray hood. He couldn't tell if it was human.

"Can you hear me?" the robed one asked.

"Loud and clear," Wang answered.

"Very good, you should have no problem standing up, then."

The robed one-stepped back, while Wang got to his feet. He stood swaying for a moment, tried to focus his eyes. Except for a slight throb in his temples, he felt all right.

"Come closer so I can study you," said the female voice.

Wang walked slowly toward the figure on the pile of blankets. Looking around, he saw he was indeed inside a tent, large enough to hold fifty people, with room to spare.

"Leave us," the female said, addressing the two who stood watching Wang.

"Are you certain?" asked one.

The female laughed. "He knows if he harms me his life would be cut short. Yes, I am certain. Send in *Gray Pebble* with a container of passion-water."

The two bowed and left through the curtain, which covered the entrance to the tent. A few moments later another robed figure entered the tent, carrying a large pitcher and two cups. "Sit beside me," the female told Wang. He realized with a start that he didn't wear any clothes.

"Where are my clothes?" he asked.

"They are being examined. We've never seen material like that. Are you cold?"

"No. I just feel better with my clothes on."

Her amused laughter appeared genuine. "You are modest. Very peculiar. Many of my own people are." She clapped her hands. The one who carried the pitcher came closer, knelt and filled the two cups. She handed one to Wang and the other one to the female. He sniffed the dark liquid inside and looked at the hooded figure on the blankets.

"Drink," she said. "You are my guest."

"Guest?" Wang chuckled. "You called me a prisoner before."

"How would you know that? Do you speak our language?"

Wang realized that the translating device made no distinction between different languages. "I speak many languages," Wang said carefully.

"Have you had dealings with my people before?"

"If you would take off your robe I might be able to tell," Wang said. "What's underneath those robes? I can't even see your face."

"I am a Naar. You do know that, don't you?"

Wang suddenly remembered Tamsy. "The girl, who came with me, told me the name of your race. Where is she?"

"She is safe. Now, join me in a cup of passion-water." She turned away and lifted her cup toward her hood.

Wang took a small sip from his cup. The liquid tasted sweet, with a bitter bite to it. Shrugging, he drained the cup. The liquid ran down his throat like raw fire. He gagged, suddenly afraid he might vomit. "Are you poisoning me?" he croaked.

"No poison," the Naar said and turned toward the robed figure who still knelt in front of them. She made a motion with one hand.

The other one rose, slim hands opened the gray robe and let it fall to the ground. Wang held his breath and stared.

The one on the blankets laughed. "What did you think you'd find underneath these robes?"

Wang felt the fire from the drink raging through his body. Between his legs, his penis stiffened, rose, engorged with blood. He kept staring at the slim figure of the naked girl who had stepped out of the loose gray robe. She smiled at him, her large purple eyes glowing softly in the semi-darkness of the tent. Sinking to the floor, she sat across from him.

"You are a Genaar female," Wang whispered.

The girl reached out and touched him. He moaned when her warm fingers curled around his stiff penis. Then she bent forward and took his penis into her mouth. Her soft, satiny tongue caressed the tip of his engorged member, and it didn't take long before he exploded inside her mouth. He wanted to pull back, but her fingers dug into his hips and pushed him down. After sucking him dry, she lifted up, her cheeks puffed. She rose, slipped into her robe and hurried out of the room.

Wang lay back into the thick blanket, his penis still stiff, the inferno inside him burning. Above him, he saw the gray robed figure of the Naar with the female voice. "What was in that drink you gave me?" he asked hoarsely, burning up with desire.

"Passion-water," she said and opened her robe.

The other Naar-female had been beautiful, but this one seemed like a vision, even Tamsy could not match her beauty. Wang looked into her eyes, surprise taking his voice away.

"Why do you stare?" she asked. "Am I not desirable?"

"You are human!" he said.

She shook her head. "I am Naar."

"But you have human eyes."

"It happens, sometimes," she said. "But only rarely."

She straddled him and put her cup to his lips. Without thinking, he swallowed the sweet liquid. "Drink," she whispered. "It will make you strong and fertile." Her hand moved to his lap, took his penis and held it. He watched as she slowly sank down, watched his penis disappear inside her belly. It was smooth, without a navel. He slid easily into her. She began to rotate her hips, her inner muscles gently gripping his hard organ. His hands moved up to cup her perfectly shaped breasts and squeezed them. She had long, thick nipples, surrounded by a rose-colored large areola.

Her lips smiled as she watched him with her black human eyes. He pulled her down, held her as he rolled with her to put her on her back. She struggled at first, but then her legs opened wide and let her knees touch the ground. Lifting up, she pulled his penis deep into her. His hands went under her buttocks and dug into their firm softness. He began to move between her widespread thighs with deep, steady strokes.

She moaned loudly, pushing up against him. He felt her warm discharge as she climaxed underneath him. Kissing her, he forced his tongue between her lips, exploring the cavity of her mouth. She tasted sweet, almost musky, but not unpleasant. When he came, his loud grunts blended with her soft cries. He crushed her to him until it was over.

Breathing heavily, he lay between her cradling thighs for a long time. When she finally pushed him off, he rolled onto his back, closed his eyes and listened to her moving away on bare feet. Without looking, he knew that she covered herself again with her gray robe.

When he opened his eyes, he saw her robed figure standing beside him, her beautiful face hidden inside the folds of the large hood.

"You have fertilized the egg I carry inside me," she said with a low voice. "It will be a beautiful child."

"Maybe I fertilized more than one egg. Maybe you'll have twins," he said with a grin.

"Impossible, since I carry only one egg."

"One egg?"

"Yes. We don't bear young, like humans. I will carry the egg inside me for a while, until it has reached sufficient size, then I will deliver it. The *Egg-Keepers* will watch over it so no harm will come to it. When the child is ready to hatch, it will break out of its shell. By then my breasts will have grown larger and will produce the nourishing fluid the child needs in the beginning."

"Is that the way your species propagates?" Wang asked.

She nodded her hooded head. "It has been so since the beginning."

"Since I will be father to your child, I think I have gained the right to know your name."

"I am Cloud-Crystal."

"And I am Wang. Tell me, the other girl, did she eat my sperm?"

"No." Cloud-Crystal chuckled. "She collected it to fertilize other eggs."

"Everybody on this... in this world seems to be obsessed with collecting sperms, or as Tamsy calls it, collecting seeds. Why is that?"

The girl shrugged. "We need them to increase the gene pool. Our numbers are low. The Xandra-born females develop eggs inside their bodies, just like the Naar. From time to time, usually at the time of the harvest festival, we capture egg-carrying females and our males fertilize their eggs. We use human males to fertilize the eggs of our females."

"That would explain your eyes. You had a human father."

"Not necessarily, but there obviously was a human male in my ancestry."

"You call yourselves *Naar*. Where do you live? Do you have cities? Villages in the forest? Do you know the history of your people?"

"So many questions at once." Cloud-Crystal laughed. "We travel far. Our home is on the southern continent. We live in the desert, where the Xandra-plant cannot grow." She drew herself up. "We do not obey the laws of the Xandra, and we do not worship her."

"Neither do I," Wang said.

"But you are traveling in the company of a Xandra-born female to the city of the Great Mother."

"Yes, I am, but not to worship. My reasons are my own." Wang sat up. "You told me that Tamsy was safe. Where exactly is she?"

"At this moment she is probably joining with one of our males, who will fertilize the egg she is carrying."

Wang felt a stab of jealousy. "I'm afraid it is too late for that. I've already had sex with her."

"You joined with her?"

Wang nodded. "That's right. Your efforts will be useless."

"If that is true, then her egg will be taken from her and destroyed. After that we will wait until another egg grows inside her."

"You can't do that," Wang protested. "That would be murder. You'd be killing my child."

"A newly fertilized egg isn't a child, yet," the Naar said coolly and clapped her hands. The curtain to the entrance parted to let a robed figure enter the tent. "You should be ready again," Cloud-Crystal said to Wang. "This is *Skyborn*. She is carrying her first egg. She has not been with a male...ever. She may be a little scared. I want you to be gentle, but I want you to give her pleasure, also. I will watch."

Skyborn came closer, shed her robe. She stood with her large purple eyes staring at Wang. Her breasts were small, underdeveloped. Wang admired her finely chiseled features, the straight nose, the pouting full lips. She came closer, sank to her knees in front of Wang. Just looking at the Naar-girl made his head spin, the effects of the passion-water had not abated yet. His penis was still hard and he wanted nothing more than plunge it into this young girl's innocent sex-organ.

Cloud-Crystal sensed his eagerness. "Take her slowly," she said with a low voice. "There is no hurry."

He touched the young Naar-girl's nubile breast and smiled when she trembled under his touch. Twirling her surprisingly large nipples between his fingers, he bent forward to take one into his mouth. He began to suck gently, but no fluid came from the breast. Running his lips along her neck, he moved to her mouth and kissed her. She responded shyly, opening her mouth to let his tongue enter. Then he pushed her onto her back and ran his hands and lips down her body, caressing every patch of her soft skin.

Reaching her genitalia, he put his lips over the puffed-up labia, probed gently with his tongue. She squirmed when his tongue entered her warm interior. She began to moan, clamped her thighs tightly against his head. At first, she tasted salty, but soon the liquid from her was sweet and pungent.

When he drew his mouth away, she tried to push his head back between her legs. He resisted and stretched out on top of her. Spreading her thighs with one hand, his stiff penis slid down her smooth belly, until he found the wet entrance he was searching.

He penetrated her without difficulties, not encountering any resistance from a membrane, which he had expected. Possibly her species differed from Humans. He didn't care. She gave a loud moan when he entered her fully and wrapped her slim legs around his torso.

The level of his own pleasure climbed almost higher than with Cloud-Crystal. Perhaps the fact that she was a virgin and this her first time, had something to do with it. It didn't matter. He moved between her widespread thighs with steady strokes, his penis hard and solid inside her tight virginal sex-sheath. She whimpered and clawed his back with long fingers, digging her heels into his buttocks. When he approached his climax, he became aware of soft hands stroking his back and sensed someone straddling him. Then hew felt a warm female body touching him, felt soft breasts flattening against his back.

With a suppressed cry, he emptied his load into Skyborn, who let out a keening, high-pitched wail.

As he pulled out of her clutching sheath, warm fingers curled around his half-erect penis, and stroked it back to solid hardness. Gentle, but strong hands pulled him off Skyborn, pushed him onto his back. A hairless, puffed-up vagina descended on top of his erect organ and sucked him inside hot moistness. When his gaze moved up, he saw slightly sagging breasts. The face he looked at was not the face he expected to see, but the face of a mature female Naar, framed by short black hair, streaked with gray.

Her purple eyes glittered in the low light. "I am *Blue-Runner*," she said with a smile and gasped as she sank back into his lap. "I am past the age of egg-carrying, but I still enjoy the process of fertilizing."

"We call it *fogging*," Wang said, grinning. For an older woman she was still a pleasure to look at and her vagina didn't feel any different from that of a young girl. Grabbing her fleshy hips, he began to slam up into her, making her cry out.

"Gentle," she whispered. "Be gentle."

He slowed down and let her take over. She moved her belly in slow, grinding motions, milking him with her strong, tight sex-organ.

A pair of warm, soft lips closed over his and a long tongue snaked into his mouth. Cloud-Crystal, the girl with the human eyes. She still wore her robe, but she had thrown back her hood. With his orgasm approaching, his body stiffened. She stopped kissing him, but hovered close, her eyes staring into his. She watched keenly as he climaxed inside Blue Runner.

When the older Naar left him, Cloud-Crystal stretched out on top of him. Her robe opened, covering both of them like a gray blanket. Then she fed his half-erect penis into her own sex-organ. He slid easily into her hot and flowing sheath.

Having climaxed several times now and feeling tired, he was content just to lie there, his hands on her small round buttocks. She squirmed above him, pressed her full breasts into his chest. He enjoyed the feel of her soft buttocks moving in his hands as she pumped her pelvis up and down.

He swam in an ocean of pure pleasure, all the while staring into her deep black eyes. When he finally came, he knew it was the last time and with a hoarse shout, he lunged up. His penis pumped its hot liquid into her and she lay quivering in his grip until he was finished, then he let go of her, totally exhausted.

With his eyes closed, he felt her leave him.

"What will we do with him?" asked the older Naar in a low voice.

"He cannot live!" Cloud-Crystal said slowly. "He knows too much about us. He asked too many questions."

The older Naar-female sighed. "He's given me great pleasure, but he cannot give me what I really want and need. Only a Xandra-born can. He is useless to me."

Chapter Sixteen

Viran had no idea where he was. Taking a deep breath, he smelled stale, musky air and when he opened his eyes, he saw darkness. As his eyes adjusted, he saw a shadow moving beside him. "Tegron?" he asked. "Is that you?"

"Who else would it be?" The big man's deep voice sounded angry.

"What happened?"

Tegron's rumbling laughter wasn't cheerful. "We are prisoners. You can't trust a Naar. I should have been on guard. I'm sorry."

"Don't be sorry. I was careless, too." Viran touched a sore spot on his shoulder. "Those little arrows could have carried a lethal poison. We could be dead."

"We may be soon."

"Is Angela with us?" Viran asked.

"I don't think so. The Naar will want to examine her. One of them is probably joined to her right now."

"I doubt that she'll mind," Viran said sourly. "What will happen to us?"

"If luck is with us we will be doing some joining ourselves. The Naar-females are very beautiful, even the old ones. They'll want you to fertilize the egg-carriers; I…well, I'll just be enjoying some passionate couplings. After that…who knows? We'll probably be killed, unless they are in need of more slaves."

"Old Grisgaar told me that the Naar are fierce warriors, but mainly they are traders. He never said they were murderers."

"The Naar are not human, my brother, nor are they Xandra-born. Who knows what they are really like? I slaved in the bowels of one of their ships, but I still know very little about them."

Sudden light flooded their prison. Viran squinted at the silhouette of the robed figure standing in the doorway.

"You will come with me!" the Naar ordered them.

Viran rose to his feet, cursed when his head hit the low ceiling. "Where are you taking us?" he asked.

"You will find out soon enough."

"Give me a moment to put on my clothes," Tegron rumbled. Turning to Viran, he said, "At least our captors had the decency to bring them along.

The Naar moved back, watched Viran and Tegron step into the light. Looking up into the sky to note the position of the sun, Viran knew it was past midday. Their prison had been a small dirt-covered hut. A number of similar huts stood close by. Only one structure was different. A huge tent. Two robed Naar guarded the entrance to.

"This is an abandoned village of the Tree-devils," Tegron whispered to Viran.

There were tall trees surrounding the small village. Viran saw horses tethered to the trees and among them walked a handful of Naar, dressed in their gray robes. He spotted Wild Spirit and Lone Walker with a feeling of hope. Having their own horses nearby, might make escaping a lot easier.

The two guards let them pass as they followed their guide into the large tent. It looked smaller from the inside, until Viran noticed the dividing wall. A group of robed Naar sat around on thick blankets. He also spotted two guards squatting in the corners, they looked as if they were meditating, but Viran knew that nothing would escape their watchful eyes.

One of the *Gray Robes* in the group turned a head and looked at Viran. He couldn't see a face inside the loose folds of the hood, but he knew it was a female Naar when she spoke. "What is your name?" she asked with a soft, velvety voice. She sounded young.

"I am called Viran, and you?"

"Call me Cloud-Crystal." She rose to her feet and came towards him. When she stood in front of him, she reached out with a slim hand and touched his biceps. "You are in excellent shape," she murmured. "An Islander, am I correct?"

"Yes, you are. I am a free man and not used to being held captive." He tried to peer into her hood, but she kept her head bent low.

She laughed. "Nobody is. But here you are." Walking over to Tegron, she put her hand on his chest. "You look human," she said, "but somehow I sense that you are not. What do they call you?"

Tegron lifted his head high. "I am Tegron. I admire your perception, *High Born*. I was human once, but now I am a creature of the Xandra."

"You address me as High-Born. You know of our customs, then. So there is more to you than it seems." She reached out with a quick movement and put her hand under Tegron's kilt. He flinched, but made no other moves.

She laughed again. "You are functional, I see. How about you, Viran? Drop those leggings of yours and let me have a look."

When Viran hesitated, she stepped up to him, undid his buckle with deft fingers and pushed his breeches down. Her long fingers curled around his limp penis, stroking it gently. When he didn't react, she chuckled. "It seems your appearance is deceiving."

"I need more than just a hand," Viran responded dryly. "I want to see more."

"So you shall." She let go of him, stepped back and lifted her robe. Viran caught a glimpse of softly curved hips, slim legs and the puffed-up lips of a female sex-organ, before the hem of the robe fell to the ground again.

He grinned. "More than that."

"That's all you're getting for now," she said harshly, turned and addressed one of the robed figures on the blankets. "Fire-Splinter, the Xandra-born is yours. You've waited a long time."

The one called Fire-Splinter rose and walked slowly toward Tegron. A thin hand appeared, long bony fingers dug into the big man's biceps. "You will give me life," a weak female voice whispered. She pulled Tegron with her. "Lie down," she told him when they reached a bed made from thick blankets. Tegron obeyed. Without being asked he removed his kilt, exposing his already half-erect organ.

The female Naar knelt beside him, fondled his penis into a stiff mast. Then the gray-robed head dipped down. Tegron's penis disappeared inside the loose folds. His body stiffened, he let out a low moan.

Viran watched with a bemused smile playing on his lips. Beside him Cloud-Crystal chuckled, then sighed. "Fire-Splinter is lucky. Not all can make the treacherous journey."

"Why? What is the matter with her?" Viran asked.

"Watch and witness the miracle of life." Cloud-Crystal said.

Tegron moaned deeply. His hands clamped around the hooded head in his lap and pushed back the hood. His eyes widened as he stared at the bald, wrinkled skull-like head. Even Viran felt revolted when he saw the old Naar-female's face. Tegron's penis was lodged deep inside her throat, her thin, loose lips worked as she sucked from his spurting organ. Then she lifted up and let his wet, glistening penis slip out of her mouth.

"Life!" she croaked. "Give me life."

Tegron pushed her from him. She fell backward and rolled off the pile of blankets. Her robe opened to display a skinny body with wrinkled skin, her flabby breasts flopping like two loose strips of cloth. "Life!" she croaked again and clawed with bony fingers. "I need life."

Before Tegron could rise, three of the other robed Naar pounced on him, pushed him against the ground and held him. The old crone discarded her robe and crawled toward Tegron.

One of the Naar, a female, had slipped out of her robe. Naked, she straddled Tegron. Lowering herself, she squatted above him and began stroking his sex-organ with skilled hands. Soon he became again stiff and solid.

It didn't surprise Viran. The Naar was young and beautiful, with a curvy slim body. Tegron's stiff mast disappeared inside her belly. Rotating her hips, she snapped her pelvis back and forth, fast and furious. While the one squatting above him assaulted his sex-organ, one of the others kissed him passionately.

The old crone knelt beside the three, her dull eyes glued to the spot where he was joined to the young Naar. With a fluid movement, the young female suddenly lifted up and Viran was surprised at the speed with which the old one took the young Naar's place. On skinny legs, she hovered for a brief moment above Tegron's strutting penis, then she sank down. The young female guided Tegron's organ into the old female's sex-channel.

A loud shriek escaped the old crone's mouth as she took the big pole inside her. Apparently unaware of the switch, Tegron lifted his hips off the floor and pushed deep into her sex-organ. Viran heard Tegron's groan as he released his fluids to pump it forcefully into the old female's womb.

"You deceived him," Viran said to the Naar standing beside him and yelped with surprise when a naked body pressed against his back and, at the same time, a soft mouth closed over his own stiff organ. Without being aware of it, he had developed an erection while watching his companion being ravaged by the old female Naar.

"So you are useful after all," a female voice whispered into his ear. Even though she had been whispering, Viran recognized her as the one who called herself Cloud-Crystal.

"I never said I wasn't," Viran groaned. He wasn't mentally prepared for this, so it didn't surprised him when a powerful orgasm racked his body moments later. When he relaxed, spent and a little disappointed at the speed things had happened, the Naar, who had sucked him off, rose and hurried away. The one behind him stepped in front of him.

He had not expected a human face.

She laughed when she saw his astonished look. "I may appear human," she said, "but I am not. Don't let the shape of my eyes deceive you, I am a true Naar."

He kept staring at her lovely body and face. Her beauty rivaled that of the Great Mother. Her breasts were perfectly shaped, her flat belly smooth, her skin without a blemish. "You have no navel," he observed. "Are you certain you are not Xandra-born?"

"Of that I am certain," she said and stepped close to him. Her breasts flattened against his chest, her breath washed warm over his face. "I've heard the Great Mother is a seductress who can give a man almost unbearable pleasure. Come, I will show you pleasures as great as hers."

She kissed him on the lips, forcing her tongue into his mouth. Then she pulled away and clapped her hands. One of the robed ones brought a pitcher and held it against Viran's lips. The liquid inside smelled sweet and pungent. Viran drank, sparingly at first.

"It is passion-water," Cloud-Crystal said. "It won't harm you."

He drank deeply, feeling the fire race through his body. His sex-organ stiffened into a thick rope. A hand grabbed his and pulled him along. One of the other females had shed her gray robe. She lay waiting on a pile of blankets, with her knees raised, her thighs apart, her pink slit beckoning.

Viran sank to his knees and moved between the girl's spread legs. When he entered her, he looked into her eyes. They were the purple eyes of a water-nymph. He moved like a man in a dream, waves of pleasure shaking his body. After climaxing inside the Naar-girl's pulsing sheath another took her place, and then another.

He found himself lying on his back, Cloud-Crystal squatting above him. Watching his pole disappear inside her descending sex-organ, he dug his fingers into her hips, lunged upwards and slipped into creamy tightness. She rode him for a long time, bringing him to an orgasm again and again. He knew he had dried up long ago, but she kept pouring sweet liquid into his mouth, her tight, velvety sheath milking him into stiffness when he thought it was not possible anymore.

Finally, she stopped playing with him and left him in a totally exhausted state. "He is an exceptional specimen," he heard her say.

"Even after fertilizing seven egg-carriers he still had the strength to pleasure me. I am satisfied."

"Even the Xandra-born has not been a disappointment," said another voice. "His powerful life-juice has given Fire-Splinter the gift of a long life. She has almost recovered from the disease."

Other voices joined in the conversation, but Viran couldn't understand what they ware saying. They spoke in a language foreign to him.

Someone pressed a cool object against his lips. He swallowed bitter liquid. It wasn't long before his mind cleared and strength flowed into his limbs. When he stood up, he found he could stand without swaying. He searched for the Naar who had fed him the liquid, but none of the Gray-Robes was near. Instead, he saw someone he had not expected to see. She stood not far from him, dressed in a soft white gown. She held a chalice in her hands.

"Great Mother, what are you doing here?" he whispered.

The Xandra smiled, the she laid a finger across his lips. "*I am not really here,*" she said. "*Only in your mind.*"

"But how...?"

"*How did I give you something to drink?*" She laughed. "*I didn't. It was an illusion. The strength came from inside you. Remember, I am part of you.*" Her expression became serious. "*Listen, Viran, they are going to kill you. You must get out of here, now! And you must save Angela, she is in mortal danger.*"

When he was about to speak she again held up a silencing finger. "*Don't talk loud, just think your questions.*"

"*How can I get away?*"

"*Tell them you have to relieve yourself. Tell them you need privacy. They will understand.*"

"*How do you know they will kill me?*"

"*The one who is called Cloud-Crystal, she gave you great pleasure, but don't let her fool you. I looked into her mind. She is cruel, she played you, Viran. You gave her more pleasure than you received. Now...go!*"

"What about Tegron?" Viran looked for his companion, found him kneeling behind one of the Naar, his lean buttocks moving slowly back and forth.

The Xandra smiled. "*He is in no danger. They need him more than they need you. For now he is safe.*" She was suddenly gone and Viran stood there, wiping his brow, wondering if he suffered from delusions.

"Go, Viran!" said the voice inside his head, and he knew he had not imagined her. He began walking toward the exit and stepped outside. One of the guards blocked his way. Viran grinned at him. "Where can I go? You know…"

The Gray-Robe shrugged. "Anywhere."

"I can't. I need my privacy. I'll just go a little way into the forest."

"Not by yourself. I'll come with you."

The Naar walked beside Viran as he headed in the direction of the trees. When they reached the edge of the forest the Naar said, "Here, you can squat down here."

Viran shook his head. "I need complete privacy. I won't go far."

Again, the Naar followed him.

"At least be descent enough and turn your back," Viran said.

After hesitating for a moment, the Naar shrugged and turned away from Viran. Without giving it much thought, Viran delivered a sharp blow to the Naar's neck. Before the Gray-Robe hit the ground, Viran caught him, took hold of his head and twisted sharply, then he let the limp body slip to the soft forest floor. He felt a stab of regret for killing someone whose face he hadn't even seen.

"It had to be done," whispered the Xandra inside his head.

"Where is Angela?" Viran asked.

"I'm not sure. She wasn't in the same place as you. I would have felt her presence. But she is in a similar shelter. She is not far; you must search for her, but hurry."

Viran looked down at his naked body. Not exactly outfitted to walk around undetected in the camp of an enemy. His gaze swept the still figure on the ground. He was bulkier than the Naar, but the robe looked loose enough to cover his body.

Before he removed the robe, he probed for the Naar's weapon, taking care in prying the blow-tube from the dead fingers. He was even more careful when he found the pouch with poisoned darts.

The robe didn't fit too badly, and he stepped out of the forest with some confidence that he might blend in with the other Gray-Robes who moved among the dirt-covered huts. Looking around, he wondered where the winged girl might be held. Remembering Angela's words, he stopped beside one of the huts, closed his eyes and tried to bring up the image of the angel. *You and I are linked, my brother,* her words echoed inside his head.

"Where are you, Angela?" he whispered.

He felt a sudden pulling in his mind, a hot, searing flash…*faces loomed above him. The sharp pain between his shoulder blades became unbearable…*

Then it was gone.

He looked past a grove of trees to his left and began walking. He saw a tent, similar to the one he had been in, hidden behind the trees. There were no guards in front of the entrance, so he walked boldly into the tent.

It was bright inside. Glowing spheres hung like miniature suns suspended from the ceiling, lighting up the interior of the tent. There were tables and shelves along the walls. On a table in the center lay a naked body…a female. A group of gray robed figures were gathering around the table, their hoods thrown back to expose their alien faces.

Recognizing the female on the table as Angela, he noticed something horribly wrong.

She had no wings.

Rage welled up inside Viran and he tore the cumbersome robe from his body. He saw Angela's sword on one of the shelves, and with a roar he leaped toward the shelve, grabbed the sword and swung it an arc above his head. Before the Naar could react to his presence, he was among them. His first stroke severed two heads from their bodies; the next split another one down to the Naar's shoulders.

Blood spattered, covering his mighty arms and torso, some of it spilled on the naked white body of Angela.

The Naar backed away. One fumbled inside his robe. Viran ran his sword right through him. Leaving it in the falling body, he pounced on the three remaining ones and smashed two heads together, dropping the limp bodies.

The last of them raced to the door and escaped.

Viran straightened his body, took a few deep breaths and looked at the carnage he had caused. It all had happened so fast, without conscious thought. Pure animal reflexes and instinct had driven him.

And rage, uncontrollable rage.

Not uncontrollable, a voice whispered inside him. *Directed. You've done well*!

He looked down at Angela. She seemed alive, her eyes were open. When he bent over her, she smiled. "Viran," she said. "You came, my brother."

"What have they done to you?" Viran asked, his voice choking.

"They cut off my wings," she whispered, tears quelling from her eyes. "They took away my life, Viran." Her lids closed over her eyes.

Viran lifted her off the table. She felt so light in his arms.

"Take me with you," a girl's voice said behind him. He turned and saw a naked girl sitting on top of another table. "I am Tamsy," she said with a shy smile. She slid off the table, walked towards him on bare feet. She was too beautiful to be human, too perfect; she could only be a Xandra-born.

"Come," Viran said.

Before he reached the entrance to the tent, the door swung open.

He stared at the gray robed figures standing in the doorway, saw the long tubes protruding from their hoods.

Chapter Seventeen

The Xandra brushed long strands of red hair out of her face and looked at Beringer. Her eyes were not human. Seeing her beside Starmote, he could not help but notice the similarity between the two women.

But at the same time, he knew that the Xandra could change the shape of her eyes any time she wanted to.

The Xandra smiled. "You are a fortunate man, Commander. I've had a long conversation with your friend here. She cares for you, you know."

"She could have fooled me," Beringer said dryly and looked at Starmote.

"Because of her and my daughter Reyna you are still alive," the Xandra said.

"Where is Reyna?"

"It is the time of the harvest festival." The Xandra waived a hand. "She is taking part in the festivities. After all, that is the reason she came here."

"What exactly is she doing?" He knew the answer, but he pretended not to know; maybe because he didn't want to.

"She is collecting seeds for me."

"Right now?"

"No. Daytime is for resting. She will tonight. You can join her, if you like. By the way, she is carrying your fertilized egg."

"My fertilized egg? I don't understand."

"There is much you don't know and understand. You remember having sexual intercourse with her?"

Beringer glanced at Starmote. He felt uncomfortable, nodded. His recollection of that night was sketchy, but he remembered the pleasure he found in Reyna's embrace. His mind had been clear for a while, his body almost healed. But the Shadow-Angel found him again that night, sucked the blood from his veins and injected him with a poisonous substance that almost killed him.

He had no hateful feelings for Naomi. She had taken, but also given. The ecstasy he found in her arms had been greater than anything he ever experienced before.

"You are right," he said. "There is much that I still need to learn. To my knowledge, the Xandra-born cannot reproduce, but I saw a little girl. The Captain called her *water-born*. Explain that to me."

The Xandra looked at Starmote, then back at Beringer. "The Genaar kept many things from you, one of them the way their species propagates. The Genaar are egg-layers, unlike humans, who carry their embryos inside their bodies until they are fully developed human beings. Small, but fully formed."

"I wasn't aware of that," Beringer said. "In other words, the Genaar are not mammalian. Why then do their women have breasts?"

"Breasts!" The Xandra smiled. "I've noticed the fascination human males have with the breasts of their females." She looked down at hers. "They are useful for many things, like feeding a small child, but grown men like to suck on them, too. You've sucked on mine, and I fed you my elixir. It gave you strength and stamina."

"The breasts of human women do not produce that elixir," Beringer said. "You haven't told me why Genaar females have breasts."

"For the same reason humans do. Once the egg hatches, the young Genaar child needs to feed just like a human baby. Since my first contact was with the Genaar, I adopted their system, except that I did modify it a little. My daughters develop eggs only every five years. They drop their fertilized eggs into water, where the young will hatch. The young are born in the water and have to fend for themselves. Only the strong survive, not many do. Children born that way are beyond my control, unless they are born under my protection in a controlled environment, like here in the City. My natural way of propagating is through the seed-pouches, and I use Humans and my daughters to multiply that way."

The Xandra smiled. "The seed-pouches are the slow way. There is another way. I can create a new living creature within hours out of my own body. You Humans call the process cloning." She pointed at Captain Cunningham. "He is such a clone. He knows that he is. Many of my creations don't."

Beringer had a sudden horrible thought. "Am I such a clone?" he asked.

Again, she smiled. "If you were, I wouldn't tell you."

"I want to know!"

"What reason would there be? You wouldn't feel any different."

"I could never father a child, for one thing."

She chuckled. "You would. I have learned." Her large alien eyes glittered. She looked at him with a solemn expression. "Much is going to change in my world."

"I'm still trying to get an understanding of your world the way it is now," Beringer said.

"I know. That is the reason you came here. You will never fully understand my world. Even though Humans live here, it is not a human world; it will never belong to you, nor will it belong to the Genaar. Starmote understands this. I hope your kind does, too." The Xandra rose to her feet, her hair spilled down to her ankles, like a red cloak. Through the veil of hair, he caught glimpses of her naked breasts, belly and thighs. She saw him look, laughed, but he detected no contempt in her laughter.

"I apologize for my delaying things," she said to Starmote, who had also risen. "We have a serious matter at hand. You explain the situation to the Commander. I will be back."

She walked past Beringer and Captain Cunningham and left through the door.

"What is this all about?" Beringer asked Starmote, who stood looking at him. When she didn't answer, he said, "Well?"

She gave him another long look, then she shrugged and pulled a small device out of one of her pockets and aimed it at one of the walls. The figure of a man appeared out of the thin air, startling Beringer. Even though he knew he was looking at a hologram, it still took him by surprise. Earth science never developed this kind of technology.

"Hello, Commander," said the smiling replica of Starfinder. The gaze of the alien's dark eyes fell on Captain Cunningham. "Hello, old friend," he said. "I see the Xandra has resurrected you. We have much to talk about. I just wish your original self would be here with us."

Cunningham smiled at the alien leader. "I am here, my friend. A little younger looking, but it is the old Captain you're looking at. By the way, you look good for a man over two thousand years old."

Starfinder chuckled. "I see, you still have your sense of humor." His expression changed, he looked at Starmote, then at Beringer. "Commander, I owe you an apology."

"For what?"

"Many things. You see, I have deceived you, intentionally. I should have insisted that you wait before you go down to the planet's surface, but you were so intent on going, so I didn't protest. Especially since I was eager myself to see what conditions we would find."

"What difference would it have made?"

"The way things are, not much, but things could have been different."

"Tell me then, how did you deceive me?" Beringer asked, wondering.

"When you left the station I considered you and your team expendable. If conditions would have warranted it, Starmote had orders to make sure you did not get back to the station." Starfinder said ruefully. "You would have done the same had you known all the circumstances. I couldn't put the lives of everybody on the station at risk."

"How many lives are we talking about?"

Again that rueful smile. "One million."

"One million?" Beringer echoed.

"One million colonists and a few hundred soldiers. All kept in cryogenic suspension."

"Can't say that I am greatly surprised. I'm just a little overwhelmed by the numbers, that's all. Why are you telling me that now?"

"We have a net of tiny satellites circling the planet. Our computer has mapped the entire planet. We've sent down probes to various locations to make closer studies, and your own experiences have given us much information. Your implanted translation devices have allowed us to monitor your every move. That is another thing I've kept from you. I'm sorry about not respecting your privacy, but the opportunity was just too good to pass up."

Beringer stood silent for a moment and let the new information sink in. He looked at Starmote. "You knew?" he asked.

She nodded. "Of course. And I would have executed my orders." Her expression was unreadable, the gaze of her black alien eyes steady on his face.

"I understand. After all, we are not really your friends, just tolerated refugees." Beringer said bitterly.

Starfinder lifted his hands away from his body. His palms faced Beringer. "You are wrong, Beringer. I do consider you my friend. I need you and you need me, as you will find out in a moment. You will have to decide where your loyalties lie and whom you will choose to be your ally. As I have told you before, we are not enemies, you and I, and I hope you remember that."

"Don't keep me in suspense," Beringer said coolly. "Just tell me what you are talking about."

"We are not alone, not anymore," Starfinder said. Behind him, another hologram appeared, this one looked like a flat black screen, in the center floated an object. A spaceship. It looked huge and menacing. "They've been hailing us; as a matter of fact, they have given us an ultimatum: Respond to their hailing within twenty Standard hours or suffer the consequences. So far we haven't responded." Starfinder looked at Beringer. "I want you to answer their attempt to contact us. Before you do, let me assure you, we are quite capable of defending the station, and we will make that clear to them."

The screen changed, a uniformed man with a hard face looked at Beringer, his dark, slanted eyes giving him a piercing stare. "So you finally decided to respond. I'm glad you're not treating our ultimatum as an empty threat."

Beringer studied the man for a moment, while trying to sort through everything that had been thrown at him since he awoke in the bed of the goddess. "Who are you?" was all he could come up with.

"I am Admiral Tamoto, commander of the Destroyer *Dragonbreath,* in the service of the *Emperor of the Mandarin Empire*, and who might you be?"

"My name is Les Beringer, Commander Les Beringer with the *Terran Space Navy.*"

"There is no Terran Space Navy, and the ship you're in has not been built by Humans. So tell me again…who are you?" The Admiral spoke harshly.

Beringer gave him a cold smile. "It is not a ship, it is a space station, and I never claimed that Humans built it."

"Then you admit that you are not human?"

"I admit no such thing. I am as human as you are and I am in fact Commander Beringer. If you know your history you will know of the Terran Space Navy."

"You are talking gibberish. Maybe I should talk to someone else. Who is that man in uniform behind you?"

Cunningham stepped forward. "I am Captain Jeremy Cunningham," he said.

"Are you the captain of that alien vessel?"

"No, I am not. Actually, I don't have a ship. My capacity as captain consisted of overseeing the colonization of the forth planet of this star system, the planet we call *Nu-Eden.*"

The admiral barked a laugh. "To colonize the fourth planet, you say? Captain Cunningham, or whoever you are, maybe you haven't noticed, that planet has already been colonized. When and how, we don't know, and it doesn't really matter. My Emperor has shown great interest in this place, and I am here to claim the planet *Dreaming Moonflower* for the Emperor. We are lifting the quarantine that has been placed upon it by overzealous and scared governments of the Alliance. From now on every living being on planet *Dreaming Moonflower* will be a citizen of the Mandarin Empire and obey the laws of the Empire."

"By what right are you claiming this planet?" Cunningham asked.

"By the *Right of Might.* Who is going to challenge us?"

"The rightful owner."

"Those few million inhabitants do not possess the military power to resist us. Our people have been studying the planet for twenty years. We've had observation stations scattered throughout the whole northern continent. Believe me, we know everything about this planet. There will be no resistance." The admiral snorted with contempt. "These people still live in the dark ages."

"You are forgetting the Xandra," the Captain said.

Admiral Tamoto smiled. "The mysterious Goddess, the so-called *Great Mother*? None of my people has ever seen her. She is just another cult-figure. She doesn't exist."

"I guess your spies are not as good as you think they are," Cunningham said and stepped aside to let a woman dressed in a dark business-suit take his place.

The admiral stared at the tall redheaded woman. Even Beringer held his breath. Her hair was short, pulled back and tied behind her head into a small knot. Large golden loops hung from her ear lobes and a necklace of sparkling round stones circled her neck. The blouse she wore under her jacket stood open to expose a deep cleavage.

Her large eyes glittered with a dark fire. She had not changed them.

"I am The Xandra," she said with a sultry voice. "I understand you want to invade my planet."

"For a goddess you don't look too impressive, just another beautiful woman, a non-human woman. You will make a good slave."

The Xandra smiled. "You are very brave up there in your tiny world you call a spaceship. You feel secure and untouchable. But don't be fooled, you are not safe from me. I know about your observation stations. I know where they are. I could take control of your men, send them back to you and destroy your ship and all your soldiers."

"You're bluffing. I'm not afraid of you."

"You should be. But since you're not afraid, you shouldn't have any problems meeting with me face to face. I could demonstrate what a goddess can do."

"My place is on the ship. Walking around on the surface of alien planets is not my job. I leave that to others."

The Xandra laughed. "Afraid after all. Let others do the dangerous jobs."

"Enough of this nonsense!" Admiral Tamoto barked. "I could burn your whole world with the push of a button. I don't think you have any idea what a destroyer of this class is capable of."

"I would advise against making any rash decisions," Beringer said. "You are forgetting about the space station."

"*What* about the station? I'll destroy it, too."

"Don't be so sure, Admiral. Attacking the station would be a fatal mistake. You are dealing with a force you know nothing about. Admiral Tamoto, let me introduce you to the Genaar." Beringer looked around for the hologram of Starfinder, but couldn't see him, so instead he pointed to Starmote. "Meet Starmote, Commander of the *Genaar Space marines.*"

Starmote gave Beringer a sidelong glance, but didn't say anything. Tamoto grinned. "You truly believe that you can intimidate me with your theatrics. First a goddess, now a commander of alien space marines. All I see is another potential female slave."

"You don't like women very much, do you, Admiral Tamoto?" Starmote spoke with a cold voice.

"They have their place." The Admiral chuckled. "As long as they are under me." His expression turned hard. "Now, let us stop wasting time." He looked at Beringer. "You convince that woman who claims to be the Xandra to tell her people not to resist the occupying forces of the Emperor land. We will set up temporary headquarters in the place they call *The City*. My spies report that location as the place where the locals worship their goddess." He smiled thinly. "That's right; I am not completely ignorant about the planet. I probably know more than you are aware of."

"Not enough as you may find out," the Xandra said with a voice that chilled Beringer to the bone. "There will be no resistance, because your forces will never set foot on my planet. I have made an alliance with the Genaar, and any hostile acts against me and my sons and daughters will be dealt with harshly. However, it does not have to be that way. I will never be the aggressor, it is not my nature, and neither will the Genaar. But let me warn you, Admiral Tamoto, attack any of us and you and your warship will cease to exist. This is no idle threat."

Beringer looked at Starmote and whispered, "Is this another performance to impress?"

Starmote gave him a little smile and shook her head. "No performance. She speaks the truth."

"Big words," Beringer heard Tamoto say. Looking back at the screen, he saw a sudden commotion behind the Admiral. "What's happening?" the Admiral barked. "Who are you? How did you get on my ship? Guards!"

On the screen, beside Tamoto, stood a familiar figure.

"I am Starfinder. I come from the space-station that you want to destroy." The alien smiled. "Put away your weapon, Admiral, it is useless against me. I am not really here."

Tamoto stepped forward and reached out. He let out a surprised grunt when his hand went right through Starfinder. "A projection!" he cursed. "Another piece of theatrics."

Starfinder was still smiling. "Check your weapon's status, Admiral."

Tamoto turned when one of his men rushed toward him. "What's the problem, Lieutenant?" he asked harshly.

The lieutenant spoke in a hushed voice. Tamoto let out another curse and turned back to Starfinder. "Is that your doing?"

"Just another piece of theatrics, that's all," Starfinder said. "If you try to use your weapons you may find that your own ship is the target."

"Impossible!" Tamoto stared at his lieutenant. "Check the computer again. Nobody has that kind of power."

"We do," Starfinder said quietly. "We Genaar never attack, but we will defend ourselves. We are an old race and we have learned from history. We prefer to live in peace with other races and I suggest you do the same, before you become obliterated by a more advanced, more warlike and ruthless enemy. And he is out there, believe me. I know that you do not represent the whole of humanity, but you can decide whether Humans and Genaar will coexist in peace or not. Our first meeting with members of the human race was favorable, let this, the second meeting, be the same."

"So what do you suggest I do, tuck my tail between my legs and go home? I could never do that. My honor is at stake."

"The fifth planet in this system will sustain life. It is a harsher place, but if you must add another planet to your Empire, why not choose that one. You will still have your honor, and your life. What good is your honor if you loose your ship and the lives of everyone on board?"

"You don't understand our ways," Tamoto said, his face suddenly without expression. He listened as his lieutenant whispered something into his ear. "We've lost communication with our people down on the planet," Tamoto said slowly, then roared with sudden rage, "You cannot do this to me! I'm loosing a battle without firing one shot!"

"You are doing all this to yourself, Admiral Tamoto. The only one fighting a battle is you," Starfinder said. "We are willing to make another concession. There are three large continents on Nu-Eden. The largest, the northern continent, belongs to the Xandra. We claim the one to the south. Our people have been living there for two thousand years. We will let you colonize the third continent, if you promise to cease all hostilities against the Xandra's people and us. Think about it, you cannot afford to turn down this offer."

The image of Starfinder disappeared. He stood suddenly back in the room, in front of the screen. The screen went blank.

Beringer stared at Starfinder. "Why was that information kept from us?" he asked.

"What information?"

"That you had colonists living on the southern continent for two thousand years. Why haven't we seen any evidence?"

Starfinder shrugged. "The evidence is there, once you know about them. These are the descendants of a thousand colonists who volunteered to settle there, because there we didn't find any signs of the Xandra. The arrival of your species a thousand years ago prevented us from finding out what happened to the experiment. But now we know. If you hadn't been in such a hurry to leave the station, you would have been told. We have much to discuss, my friend, when you come back to the station. But first we must deal with the warship and other matters."

"It seems to me that you have made some kind of deal with the Xandra, of which I know nothing about, either," Beringer said. "I'd like to know: how do the human inhabitants fit in?"

"Anyone who doesn't seek conflict with me and my sons and daughters has nothing to fear," the Xandra said. "Starfinder will deal with his people. I would like your help to resolve the situation that exists with Numerika and with the Amaarins. I don't want to deceive you, Beringer. The Genaar were the first to settle on my world, I identify with them. Starfinder has promised me protection against the threat from the Humans. I would prefer that we come out of this without bloodshed. A peaceful existence between our species would be of great benefit to all of us."

"I agree," Beringer said, slowly. "I'll do what I can."

Chapter Eighteen

Staring up at the gray ceiling of the tent, Wang realized he had been asleep. Even knowing that he may die soon had not been enough to keep him awake. He felt rested. When he looked around, he saw that he was not alone. A couple of robed Naar squatted not far away, watching him. He couldn't tell if they were males or females.

"I wish you people would wear different clothes, so I knew if I looked at a man or a woman," he said to one of them. "I guess you've never heard of fashion. Speaking of clothing, I wouldn't mind getting back my own. It's getting chilly in here."

"Cover your body with a blanket," one of the Naar said.

"By the sound of your voice you are a man. Tell me, is your society run by women? It seems to me they make all the decisions."

"Our females occupy high places in the hierarchy," the Naar replied, "but they do not make all of the decisions."

Wang looked thoughtfully at the Naar who seemed willing to talk. "My name is Wang," he said. "I am a stranger to your world, but I am not alone. I have friends who will miss me. I overheard Cloud-Crystal and Bluerunner talking. I think they want me dead. Am I correct?"

The Naar shrugged. "If they decided that then it shall be."

"It would be a mistake. My friends would take terrible revenge," Wang said. "Why do they want to kill me, anyway? I have done nothing to threaten or harm you. Cloud-Crystal has taken my seed into her and I've fertilized the eggs of a number of other females."

"Your friends will not find us. We come in secrecy and we leave in secrecy, that is how we survive, and that is why you must die. The less is known about us, the safer we are."

"You are talking too much, Sand-Runner," the other Naar spoke up, also a male.

"No harm is done," Sand-Runner said.

Wang stood up and stretched. "While you two argue, I need to go for a walk," he said and began walking toward the only entrance he could see.

Both Naar came to their feet with fluid motions. "We have orders to keep you in here," Sand-Runner said.

"I just need to stretch my legs and get some fresh air. It stinks in here." He had reached the two Naar. Before they could react, his foot came up and smashed into the head of the second one, knocking him to the ground. Then he grabbed the one called Sand-Runner and pinned his arms behind his back. He pulled the hood off the Naar's head to expose his face.

"As I suspected," Wang said. "You're just a boy."

Sand-Runner struggled in Wang's grasp. Looking down at his fallen comrade, he asked, "Did you kill him?"

"He's alive. I have no reason to kill anyone. But I will, if I'm threatened," Wang warned. "I'm going to release you. I want you to take off your robe--and do it carefully; I don't want to hurt you. Nod, if you will comply."

Sand-Runner nodded. Wang let go of him, stepped back and watched the Naar slip out of his gray robe. Like the females, Sand-Runner looked quite handsome, with a well-built, muscular body. He stared at Wang with his large alien eyes. "Now what?" he asked.

"Now you undress your friend," Wang ordered him.

The other Naar appeared older, his body thinner, leaner. Wang bent over him to see if he was breathing and was satisfied to see the rhythmic movement of the Naar's deep chest. He had made the right choice in attacking the older Naar first. Wang discovered a thin, long tube in the Naar's hand.

"These darts?" Wang asked Sand-Runner. "Does the poison kill?"

Sand-Runner shook his head. "No, just puts you to sleep."

Wang bent down to pull the blow-tube from the Naar's grip. "Turn around," he told Sand-Runner. The young Naar obeyed slowly. He collapsed when the small dart hit him in the shoulder. Wang found a pouch that contained more of the darts. Carefully he inserted one into the end of the blow-tube, and then he shot it into the older Naar's thigh.

Sand-Runner's robe fit him quite well, the only problem seemed to be the hood, he found it difficult keeping the loose folds from falling over his eyes. He kept the blow-tube and stuffed the pouch with the arrows into one of the robe's deep pockets. Then he carefully pulled apart the flaps that covered the door. The room he stepped into lay in semi-darkness, he recognized it as the one he had been in before. A group of hooded Naar sat in the far corner, and another against the wall toward the middle.

He caught movement in the other corner and when he looked, he saw a big, muscular man lying on his back, a naked female Naar writhing in his lap. Wrinkled skin covered her bony body and her breasts hung like flat strips of cloth in front of her thin chest. Judging by her gray hair she was obviously quite old, but she moved her hips with great vigor in the big man's lap.

Nobody paid him any attention, so he walked briskly toward the exit. He past two guards outside, but they didn't say anything.

It was daylight outside, he figured late afternoon. Looking around, he saw the horses at the edge of the forest. His first impulse told him to get a horse and ride the hell away from here, but he knew he couldn't do that. He had no idea where he was, and he wasn't a woodsman who could find his way out of a deep forest. Besides, he had to find Tamsy, his clothing and his gear. Once in possession of his things, he could call the shuttle for help. In order not to arouse any suspicion he couldn't waste time looking around, so he strode purposefully toward a grove of trees.

He found himself in a huge, natural clearing, surrounded by thick forest. The large dirt-covered mounds reminded him of the termite mounds on his home planet, but then he noticed the small openings and realized that they were some kind of dwelling. Too small though for normal sized humans, or even Xandra-born.

He encountered a group of the Gray-Robes beside a grove of trees; they were talking in hushed voices, obviously discussing something. He hesitated for a moment, looked around and saw another tent behind the trees. Taking a sharp turn, he began walking toward the tent, hoping that Tamsy might be held in there. He didn't think they'd put her into one of the small huts.

He hadn't gone far when the door to the tent opened and one of the Gray-Robes came storming out, yelling with a loud voice. His hood was thrown back, exposing his head, and Wang saw that the Naar was old. The group of Naar Wang had past broke up. Some of them ran toward the old Naar, the others toward the tent Wang came out of. Wang found himself soon surrounded by a half dozen Gray-Robes, leaving no choice but to join them.

He hadn't quite understood what the old Naar had yelled. Something about someone gone mad, decapitated heads and blood. The old Naar had been upset and almost incoherent.

The group reached the open door to the tent to be confronted by a naked blood-covered savage, carrying a nude girl. She seemed unconscious. Looking into the tent, Wang saw several of the Gray-Robes lying on the floor, and blood everywhere.

Then he saw Tamsy. She stood behind the savage. Wang wanted to call out to her, but realized that she wouldn't recognize him in the gray robe, and he couldn't risk exposure.

The savage roared when the Naar cut off his escape. He moved backwards, toward the table in the middle of the room. Wang saw the bloody sword on it. But before the savage reached the table his legs buckled under him, he fell to the floor, with the girl he carried sliding on top of him. Her body turned and Wang saw two bloody stumps protruding from her back.

Tamsy cowered on the floor beside the still body of the savage. Wang could hear her soft whimpering.

A sudden noise erupted outside the tent. Two of the Gray-Robes, who had not been able to enter, were suddenly flung backwards into the room. Over their bodies stepped a black-clad figure, his head covered by a full helmet that hid his face behind darkened glass. He carried a laser rifle in his hands. Another, more massive and larger figure, similarly dressed, appeared in the doorway, stepping over the bodies on the floor into the room. Behind him came three more.

The first one swatted at something in the air with a gloved hand. "Stop wasting those ridiculous arrows," he growled and faced the Gray-Robes. The one behind him held a device in his hand, which he moved, in a slow arc in front of him.

"This thing says he is in here, but I don't see him," a familiar voice said.

Wang threw back his hood. "If you are looking for me, you've found me," he said louder than intended.

The one with the device swung his covered face around to look at Wang. "You're out of uniform, Lieutenant," he said and opened his faceplate.

"So are you, Sergeant. Where the hell did you get those outfits? They're certainly not standard Service Issue."

Sergeant Stasnowsky grinned. "A gift from the Genaar. So is this little tracer. Without it, we would never have found you."

"Somebody sure did a number in here, by the looks of things," said the man who had come in first. Wang recognized his voice; it belonged to marine Cameron Sisco, a man well suited for this mission.

"It must have been the savage. Isn't that the guy Lambert rescued?" Stasnowsky asked.

"How do you know all that?" Wang asked.

The sergeant gave him an apologetic grin. "It's that little device the Genaar put into your skull, Lieutenant. It's more than just a translator. We've been monitoring your progress on the planet. It was like we were there with you guys. Everything you did was displayed in a hologram; real lifelike, too. These Genaar, they sure have some advanced technology."

Wang stared at the Sergeant. "You mean you saw everything we did?" he asked.

Stasnowsky nodded. "Pretty well, sir."

"How?"

"Through your eyes and ears."

"Who was watching this?"

"Just me and Lt. Conelli, sir, and the Genaar."

"You two can exchange pleasantries later," said a female voice. It came from one of the last three who had entered the room. She sounded a little like Starmote.

"Who is she?" he asked.

"One of the Genaar-soldiers Starfinder revived," Stasnowsky explained. "She's right. We should move out."

"Give me a moment," Wang said and turned to look at Tamsy who was still crouching beside the fallen savage. "She's coming with us," he said.

"I understand," Stasnowsky nodded and grinned. "Your little playmate." Then he added, "I'm sorry, sir, I didn't mean it that way."

Wang waved him off. "It's alright, Sergeant. I haven't been myself ever since I've landed on this planet, and neither have the others, except maybe Starmote."

"How about the big guy and the girl with the stumps?" asked marine Sisco. "She'll need medical attention."

"We'll take them with us," the Sergeant said. "See if you can revive him."

"Let me do it," said the female soldier. She walked over to the naked man on the floor and bent over him. Tamsy backed away from her.

"Tamsy," Wang called to the Xandra-girl and walked toward her. She stared at him with frightened eyes and suddenly recognized him. "Wang!" she cried out and flung herself into his arms.

Wang stroked her hair and lifted her tearstained face. "It's alright," he murmured, "you're safe now."

One of the standing Naar backed against a wall and spoke up suddenly, "Who are you?" he asked with a voice that didn't sound too steady.

Stasnowsky gave him a glaring stare. "We are gods from the stars," he growled, "and we've come to adjust a wrong that has been committed here."

"The Islander has done all this," the Naar complained. "He's killed our healers."

"They're not healers, they are butchers. Look at what they've done to the angel. They have amputated her wings," Wang said sharply.

On the floor, the unconscious savage stirred. The Genaar soldier, who knelt beside him, pocketed the device she had held against his neck.

The man opened his eyes, tried to sit up, but was hampered by the unconscious angel who still lay on top of him.

"We're friends," the Genaar soldier said, "we'll get you away from here."

While Sisco covered the robed Naar, the other two soldiers lifted the injured angel off the savage who came slowly to his feet. He swayed for a moment, then he looked around with narrow eyes. "I am Viran," he said. "I know who you are and I thank you for your help." He pointed to the unconscious girl on the floor. "She is Angela, and a favorite of the Mother. We must take her to the City, where she will be restored."

"All in good time, Viran," said the female Genaar. "We will treat her temporarily, and then we have to take care of another matter. She'll be alright."

Viran looked at her. "The Xandra thanks you, Genaar. I will help you with that other matter, but you must also rescue my companion, Tegron. He is still with the Naar-females. Once they're done with him they'll probably kill him."

"Show us the way to your companion," the Genaar said.

Chapter Nineteen

Lambert watched Vienne and then Mirtin climbing back into the shuttle. Before he could give the computer the command to close the exit, a figure, dressed in a clinging, black outfit came up the ladder and jumped through the door. Aiming a weapon at Lambert's head, the intruder said with a harsh male voice, "Anyone moves and he is a dead man!"

Behind him two more dark-clad figures appeared.

"There are more of my men outside your vehicle," said the first man, "but just in case you get any stupid ideas…" His hand moved and a bright stream of energy hit the instrument panel of the shuttle. The stench of melting plastic filled the air. The lights dimmed and flared back to life as the emergency power cut in. The man grinned, aiming his weapon back at Lambert. "I think I've just stranded you on this forsaken place," he said.

"You yellow son of a dog," Mirtin cursed from between clenched teeth.

The man looked at her. His slanted eyes became tiny slits. "So you speak my language. Are you an escaped slave of the Empire?"

"I am Captain Koyo. I serve the Alliance," Mirtin said in a defiant tone.

"Well, Captain Koyo, from now on you'll be in the service of the Emperor. This planet is now part of the Mandarin Empire. If you can proof that your bloodline hasn't been diluted too much you might even get back your rank. You're friends here," he waved his free hand, "they are prisoners of war."

"I wasn't aware that there was a war," Massater said.

"We've always been in a state of war," the man said. "Now, let's go! You first," he said to Lambert.

It was dark outside now. Only the red moon illuminated the path they followed through the thick forest. The enemy camp wasn't far away. There were two shuttles hidden under the branches of the tall trees. They must have been already there long before Lambert and his passengers arrived, otherwise the computer would have detected them, unless they possessed cloaking devices.

The temporary shelter Lambert saw, confirmed his assumption about the camp having been there for quite some time. His captors led him to one of the shelters and pushed him inside.

The walls and ceiling glowed with a dim light, but still bright enough to make him squint. There were no furnishings, except for one chair and a small desk. Before Lambert had a chance to examine anything else, the door opened and two people entered.

Two women.

"So you are the prisoner," one of them said.

Lambert shrugged. "If you say so."

"You don't think your situation is serious, don't you?" the other woman said.

"You tell me," Lambert said.

The first woman moved the chair into the center of the small room. "Sit!" she told Lambert.

He complied, looked expectantly at his two captors. "If you are planning to torture me, I must warn you that I have been conditioned. You will get nothing out of me, unless I volunteer to do so."

One of them laughed. "We don't torture prisoners. There are other ways to extract information. What is you name?"

"John Lambert. Space-marine. Serial Number..."

"Never mind that." The woman waved her hand impatiently. "All I want is your name. May I call you John?"

Lambert shrugged again, grinned. "If it makes you happy."

"We're wasting time," said the other woman. "Hook him up." She pulled something out of her pocket, stepped up to Lambert and touched his temples. It stung for a moment, them he felt nothing. He watched the woman put a small device onto the desk. It began to glow. Moments later a screen appeared above it.

"A truth-detector," she explained. "Tell me again: what is your name?"

"Still John Lambert."

"Very good. Are you with the Alliance?"

"No. I am in the Service of the Terran Space Navy."

"The what?"

"The Terran Space Navy."

"There is no such thing as the Terran Space Navy."

"He speaks the truth," said the woman who watched the screen.

"Either your detector is faulty, or he really is conditioned."

"There is nothing wrong with my detector. Maybe he is telling the truth."

"How can that be? I've never heard of the Terran Space Navy. Have you? I think we have a spy on our hands, deeply conditioned to resist any probing."

"You could save yourselves a lot of time if you just believe me," Lambert volunteered. "I have nothing to gain by lying to you."

"Shut up, prisoner! We'll have to try another approach. Get undressed!" the woman, who had interrogated him, commanded.

Lambert stood up and removed his clothes. Naked, he sat down again, shivering for a moment when the cold plastic of the chair touched his buttocks. He looked with a bemused expression at the two women.

"Are you human?" his interrogator asked.

Laughing, Lambert spread his arms. "Look for yourself. Everything is normal. What about you two? I can see that you are women, those tight outfits leave nothing to the imagination, but are you human women?"

"Of course we are human. Even if we weren't, we are not the prisoners."

"Why is it so damn hot in here?" asked the one watching the small screen on the desk. The other one wiped her brow. "Because the air-conditioning unit isn't working. We always have to deal with inferior products. Why do you think nobody wants to join the *Phase-one* teams?"

"You talk as if we had a choice. Open the door a little, bring in some fresh air."

Lambert watched the woman walk to the door, admired the play of her plump buttocks under the tight material of her pants. Cool air entered the cabin. Lambert detected a familiar scent and took a few deep breaths. He felt a gentle flutter in his groin. "You never told me your names," he said.

"I am Nance and she is Cim," said the one who had opened the door.

"He doesn't need to know our names!" Cim said sharply.

"Sorry." Nance bowed her head slightly. She seemed to be the younger of the two.

"Well…Nance and Cim, what else do you want to know?" Lambert felt a little lightheaded. The scent of the purple flowers seemed to become stronger.

"Quiet, prisoner John! We will be doing the talking," Cim said.

"Go right ahead." Lambert grinned. "Tell me, then. What are you people doing on this lovely planet?"

Cim put her face close to Lambert's. "I don't think you realize your position. Maybe it is time you take us seriously."

"Oh, I'm taking your seriously," Lambert inhaled deeply, the slightly musky smell of her feminine body and the scent of the flowers from outside made him want to grab her and kiss her. She had full, sensuous lips. He sensed the suppressed passion in this woman. Her slightly flaring nostrils quivered as she stared into his eyes.

Pulling away abruptly, she opened the top of her tight outfit. She turned to Nance and said, "I don't know about you, but I am unbearably horny."

"So am I. I've been like this ever since we landed," Nance replied. Her face seemed flushed, her breathing unsteady.

Lambert grinned. "Maybe I can help," he volunteered.

Cim stared at him. "Help with what?"

"Well…your condition. You know."

The woman stared at him. "You shouldn't have understood that. How do you know our language?"

Damn! Lambert cursed himself. It could have been to his advantage had they continued to believe that he couldn't understand them. That happened to be one of the drawbacks with the translator in his skull. One never knew what language was actually spoken.

"I have a gift for languages," he said.

"That is the first lie you've told us," Nance, who had been watching the monitor, said.

"It doesn't matter." Cim waved her off. Her chest heaved with her increased breathing. "We were told to extract information from him, by any means we deem necessary. I believe this is necessary." She removed the wide belt she wore around her slim waist, and then she slipped out of her clothes.

Lambert watched her peel off her tight outfit. The sight of her creamy breasts tumbling out made him catch his breath. Her waist was narrow, her hips round and smooth. Below her flat belly, a small black triangle covered her genitals. Her hand reached down, took hold of his half-erect penis and began stroking it. It didn't take much for Lambert to become exited and fully erect. He groaned when she straddled him. She cried out softly when his hard penis slid into her creamy tight sheath.

"Ahh…" she moaned loudly and began snapping her pelvis back and forth. "Now you will tell me everything you know," she gasped. "Everything."

Lambert put his hands on her solid buttocks and dug his fingers deep into their soft flesh. "Whatever you want to know," he groaned, clenching his teeth to keep himself from exploding too soon inside her hot inferno.

"Don't let him come." Nance's voice sounded breathless and tight beside Lambert's ear. "Remember…you are torturing him."

Cim cried out, her hot discharge ran down Lambert's inner thighs as a powerful orgasm shook her body. "Don't worry," she breathed. "It won't happen."

"Maybe I should interrogate him for awhile," Nance said.

"Alright." Cim lifted up, freed Lambert's penis. He looked at Nance, who stood naked in front of him. It was more obvious now that she was younger than Cim, also thinner. Her breasts were firm, but small, her hips narrow, juvenile. Straddling him, she took hold of his erect penis and guided it toward her nearly hairless vagina. She took him effortlessly into her wet sheath.

He buried his face between her small breasts and began licking her skin. The salty taste of sweat lingered on his tongue, not unpleasant. Her narrow hips moved furiously in his lap and her sheath slid over his shaft with a tight, powerful grip. He tried to hold back, but the speed of her whipping sex-organ made him lose his control. With a loud groan, he let go and erupted inside her sucking channel. The woman quivered in his lap and milked every drop from his pumping penis.

When he stopped gushing, she relaxed in his arms, sighing deeply. "I needed that badly," she whispered and began to rotate her pelvis. Lambert was still lodged inside her, hard and solid.

"You're quite stubborn, aren't you?" she breathed. "I guess you need to be punished a little while longer."

The door was suddenly flung open. Lambert stared at the male soldier who stormed in. "What is going on here?" the soldier demanded to know and gave Nance a push. She toppled off Lambert's lap.

"You were told to interrogate the prisoner, not fuck him!" the soldier roared. He slapped Lambert across the face. "You'll pay for this, you white dog!" He turned toward the women. "Get dressed, both of you. We'll talk about this tomorrow."

With that, he stalked out of the room.

"I guess the interrogation is over," Lambert said and rubbed his cheek.

"You're lucky we were interrupted," Cim said, "I was ready to give you a real good punishment."

"Too bad." Lambert grinned. "I could have used some more punishment. You two are a couple of really skilled interrogators."

The two women dressed and told Lambert to do the same. Nance grabbed him by the arm and marched him outside. The red moon had disappeared. This was the darkest time of the night, but it would soon be daylight.

"What's going to happen to us now?" Lambert asked Nance.

"That is up to the commander of our mission," Nance answered. "I'm afraid it doesn't look good. He doesn't like people of your kind. As for myself, I have nothing against you. I am just doing my job."

"That is good to know," Lambert said dryly.

They passed one of the shuttles. Lambert stopped to study it more closely. There were markings that looked like some sort of writing on the side, but he couldn't read it. Sleek and streamlined, the shuttle was meant for speed in the atmosphere of a planet.

A soldier came out of the exit door, looked up and saw Lambert and Nance standing there. "Where are you taking the prisoner?" he bellowed. Lambert recognized him as the one who led the team who captured them.

"I'm taking him back to the other prisoners," Nance said.

"I told you to interrogate him, soldier!"

"We did interrogate him already, Major," Nance said.

"Have your report on my desk in the morning," the Major barked. "Now…take him back into confinement and extract more out of him!"

Nance saluted. "Yes, sir. Will do." She grabbed Lambert's arm. "Back to your cell, prisoner John!" she said sharply.

Once back inside the little shelter Nance locked the door and turned toward Lambert. "You heard the Major. I have to interrogate you some more," she said. "Get undressed, and hurry, we don't have much time."

Lambert grinned, removed his clothing and watched Nance do the same. Naked, she knelt on the floor. Arching her back, she smiled up at him. "What are you waiting for?" she asked softly. He dropped to his knees behind her. Looking at her small round buttocks and the puffed-up lips of her vagina squeezed between her slim thighs, it didn't take much coaxing for him to achieve an erection.

Guiding his stiff member between her spread thighs, he put the swollen head of his penis into the pink slit and pushed. With a soft groan, he slid easily into the tight sheath.

Crying out, she pushed back, taking him deep into her. She bucked violently underneath him as he pumped back and forth. His hand stroked her smooth back and grabbed her hips to steady his movements.

"Oh... Ohh... I'm coming!" she cried. He felt her contractions as she milked his penis. When she calmed down, he moved his hands to her chest, cupped her small breasts and squeezed them gently.

He pulled out of her and turned her around. She lay on her back, legs wide open and stared at him out of half-closed eyes. Kneeling between her spread thighs, he studied her slim body, ran his hands over her flat belly and touched her smooth mons pubis. She smiled lazily, reached toward him, curled her fingers around his penis and stroked it gently.

"Put it back in," she whispered.

Taking his time, he moved forward, lifted her hips and pushed his stiff mast slowly into her. She began to move her hips, but her movements were restricted by the position they were in. Lambert pulled out, stretched out on top of her, then he entered her again. With forceful strokes, he moved between her clutching thighs, bringing her to several orgasms, before he gave in to the powerful pounding in his loins.

His lips closed over hers and he was surprised when she responded with great passion. With a shout, he erupted inside her. He held her tight until he felt empty and the throbbing of his penis subsided.

She kept her tongue inside his mouth and with her hands she held his head so he couldn't move away. Realizing she was still in the throes of her own climax, he pushed his erect penis deep into her. Her quivering and pulsing soft sheath milked him furiously. Then she collapsed underneath him and let go of his head. Her breath came in short gasps, bathing his face with hot air.

"My major told me to extract more information out of you," she said and giggled. "I guess I extracted as much as you can give me." She kissed him on the nose. "Now, let's get dressed in case someone comes to check up on us."

They barely managed to finish dressing when somebody knocked on the door. Nance opened the door to let in Cim.

"Why did you lock the door?" Cim asked and looked at Nance with narrow eyes.

Nance shrugged. "It is safer that way."

"What happened in here?" Cim asked and sniffed. "There is a strange odor in here."

"Like I said before, the air-conditioning unit isn't working," Nance said.

"The Major wants to see you," Cim told her. "I'll watch the prisoner."

After Nance left, Cim locked the door behind her. "Alright," she said and began stripping off her clothes. "Time for some more interrogation. Get naked!"

He had barely enough time to push down his pants when she shoved him so hard he landed on his back, and then she straddled him. He felt her slit rub his penis and it didn't take long for him to sprout a huge erection. Then he slid into her. Feeling a bit tired from his bout with Nance, he lay back and watched Cim's naked body writhing above him. Her breasts were larger than Nance's and they wiggled deliciously as she bounced up and down.

Her almond eyes stared into his, but he wasn't certain if he even saw him. She opened her mouth to let out a cry as she experienced her first orgasm. In a way, she looked sexier than Nance, with her wider and fleshier hips, and she acted more aggressively. Somehow, it turned him on immensely.

When her body finally began to sag, he pulled her down, turned to put himself on top of her. She opened her eyes in surprise, then she spread her legs wide, and with renewed vigor, she moved against him.

He fucked her long and hard until she whimpered for him to stop, then he erupted with tremendous force inside her clutching organ.

Insistent banging against the closed door made him pull out and jump up. "I think someone wants to come in badly," he said, trying to catch his breath.

Chapter Twenty

Mirtin was angry with herself for not being alert and with John Lambert for not doing his job. His instruments, primitive as they were, should have detected the presence of their captors. She looked around their small prison. Four bare walls. There were some things piled up in a corner. Obviously, they were inside a storage shed.

"What's going to happen to us?" Vienne asked.

Mirtin shrugged. "They'll probably interrogate us, one by one, and then they might just shoot us."

"Why would they do that? We've done nothing to them. That would be a hostile act. The Alliance would retaliate."

"Wake up, girl. Do you really think the Alliance would risk a war because of a small incident like that? We are not important enough. Besides, who would know? The moment we landed on this planet we were considered expendable." Mirtin gave a little laugh. "You know, my father was right, I should have declined this mission."

"Stop this, you two!" Massater said angrily. "If they wanted us dead they would have killed us already."

"I wonder why they separated Lambert from us. He doesn't know anything about this planet," Vienne mused.

"They don't know that." Mirtin stared out of the small window that let some diffused light into the shed. The red moon illuminated the two Landers. They weren't the usual exploration vehicles. These were fighter craft, fast and deadly. As equally efficient in space as in the atmosphere of a planet. That meant only one thing...somewhere out there lay a war ship of the Mandarin Empire.

Her own dive-ship was hidden in one of the craters on the red moon. Much good did it do her now, not that it mattered. With Lambert's shuttle permanently grounded, they'd never get off this planet anyway.

"We should try to escape," she said. "I don't see any guards."

"They'll have a cordon of micro-sentries set up all around this camp," Massater said. "We wouldn't get very far."

"We could try."

"Forget it. I don't feel like getting fried while trying an escape that is doomed to fail. Let's just wait."

"Wait? For what? For rescue? Nobody knows we are here." Mirtin was itching to do something. "I hate it when I'm not in control."

Massater chuckled. "So that's the problem. I'll bet you don't take orders well, Captain Koyo."

"I don't. I give them!"

The door flew open. One of the black-clad soldiers stood in the doorway. He pointed a weapon at Mirtin. "You!" he said. "The Commander wants to talk to you."

"Do I have a choice?" Mirtin asked with a defiant tone.

"None. Now--move!"

Mirtin tried to engage the soldier in conversation as she walked in front of him, but he told her to shut up. He led her to one of the Landers, where another soldier waited at the open exit-door. He waved her inside. It took a moment for her eyes to adjust to the bright light. The cabin looked Spartan. Benches along two of the walls, a swivel chair against another in front of a large screen.

The chair was occupied.

"So you're the half-breed prisoner I was told about." The man appeared muscular, bulky, and larger than most of his race.

Mirtin drew herself erect. "I don't consider myself a half-breed. My bloodline is as pure as yours."

The man chuckled. "Proud, too. I am Commander Lin Ko. And you are?"

"Captain Mirtin Koyo."

The Commander leaned forward. "Well…Captain Koyo. What are you doing on this planet?"

"That is classified, Commander Ko."

"I could have you shot as a spy, Captain!"

Mirtin gave a short laugh. "A spy? Neither one of us should be here. This is a closed system, I'm sure you are aware of that."

"I have news for you, Captain Koyo. This planet is part of the Mandarin Empire. It is not a closed system to us."

"It has never been part of the Empire and it will never be. There is a reason why this system is closed." Mirtin said sharply. "Until we find out what makes this place tick it will stay closed. I've been here for months and I still don't know what dangers we are actually facing. And the dangers are here, believe me. The whole of humanity may be threatened."

"There is nothing here that we can't deal with." Commander Ko leaned back in his chair. "Our weapons are superior to anything we may come up against. We've had our spies here, also, probably for much longer than the Alliance. The inhabitants of this planet are pre-technical. Admittedly, there exist a few things we cannot explain, but there is no great threat here."

"The Alliance will not sit idle and let you just invade this planet," Mirtin said.

"Who will take a stand against us? The Alliance? The rest of the colonies? Face it, the fleet of the Empire is the most powerful force in this sector of the Galaxy, and there is nobody who will oppose us."

"I don't think it is the Alliance you have to worry about, Commander. You may just loose your teeth right here on this planet."

"If there is anything you can enlighten me with, let's hear it."

"Anything I know is classified."

"We can extract information quite easily."

Mirtin smiled. "I am surprised, Commander. You should know that I am conditioned."

"Against pain?"

"My system will shut down."

"You must be very important, not just a regular operative. Interesting. Makes me wonder. Again--what are you doing here?"

"Gathering information, for the good of humanity. That includes you, believe it or not. As I told you before, there is more under the surface than appears to be. You'd do well to heed my warning."

"A threat?"

"A warning, well-meant."

The Commander stood up and stretched. His muscles rippled under his skin-tight outfit. The gaze of his dark eyes lingered on Mirtin. "You've been here for the better part of a year, Captain, tell me: what the hell is in the air? My men are going crazy. They all act like a bunch of sex-starved maniacs. Myself..." he stopped and stared at Mirtin.

"Yes, Commander?" Mirtin asked. She knew what he wanted to say.

"There are women in my outfit, but I am their superior. I cannot afford to engage in activities with them that would definitely undermine my authority."

"What are you saying?" Mirtin pretended not to understand. She felt a sudden flush in her cheeks, below her belly a gentle pulsing.

Commander Ko turned and ran his hand over the screen on the wall behind him. It sprang to life, displaying a three-dimensional image of a naked man in a chair. In his lap, facing him, sat a woman, also quite naked, leaving no doubt to what she was doing. Her buttocks pumped with furious speed and her loud moans came clearly over the speakers.

"That's how my female soldiers interrogate prisoners," Commander Ko said. He made no effort to hide his sarcasm.

The picture was large and clear enough for Mirtin to recognize the man in the chair. Behind Lambert stood another woman, also naked.

"Explain this whole thing to me!" the Commander demanded.

Mirtin shrugged. "Like I said, it is in the air." The throbbing inside her vagina was almost uncontrollable.

Commander Ko darkened the screen, walked to the door and locked it. He turned back to Mirtin, his face unreadable. "I will interrogate you now, prisoner Koyo," he said, stepped up to her and kissed her. His hands opened the top of her camouflage outfit and fumbled with her breasts.

Mirtin sighed deeply, pushed down her pants and unlocked his belt. Freeing his erect member, she curled her fingers tightly around it and stroked it. Sinking to her knees, she touched it with her lips, licking it with her tongue. Then her lips slipped over the swollen head. Sucking the large and hard organ into her mouth, she could barely wait to take it into her aching vagina.

Ko pulled out of her mouth, stepped back and removed his clothing. Mirtin admired his bulging muscles, his rippling flat belly, but especially his erect massive penis. She stripped off her own clothes and stood naked in front of her captor.

"You're big," she said.

He chuckled. "I'm sure you can take it," he said and pulled her to him. She put her arms around his neck, wrapped her legs around him. He put his hands under her thighs and lifted her up, then he began pushing his organ into her slippery sheath. There was some resistance for a moment, and then he slid slowly into her. She cried out, but it wasn't because it hurt. He walked with her until her back pressed against the wall, and then he fucked her with slow, but deep thrusts.

She clung to him, pushing her breasts into his hard chest. He filled her completely; her vagina walls molded themselves snugly around his thick organ. Without uncoupling he turned, sank to his knees. Then he bent forward and put Mirtin onto her back. She pulled up her legs until they touched her shoulders and took him even deeper into her belly.

He was a big, powerful man and capable of hurting her. She was his prisoner. Yet, he moved gently and with slow, steady strokes between her wide-open thighs. He kept it up for a long time, brought her to tremendous orgasms several times. Then his breathing became labored. Stiffening, he let out a suppressed shout. She lowered her legs and dug her heels into his quivering buttocks. Inside her, his organ jumped and began to throb, she felt his hot discharge shoot into her womb. Then he lay on top of her, breathing hard. With a stab of regret, she let him pull out of her.

She looked up at him as he stood above her. "I guess you've discovered my weakness," she said. "I was never conditioned against this kind of interrogation."

"And I was never really taught how to be an expert at it," Commander Ko smiled.

"With that weapon of yours you are an instant expert," Mirtin said.

He looked down at his member. Even in its half-erect state it looked still quite imposing. "I know I'm well endowed," he said. "It can be a problem sometimes. Did I hurt you?"

"No, but it was a tight fit." Mirtin smiled. "My little flower here is quite adjustable."

Commander Ko studied her for a while. "You know," he said. "You have an aura about you that attracts me to you. We could work something out. I'd like to have you on my side. Let's face it, you don't owe the Alliance anything; they left you here to rot. I would never do that to any of my soldiers and neither would the Emperor. You could work for us."

Mirtin sat up, looked into his eyes. "Would you do it?" she asked solemnly.

He smiled and shook his head.

"Then you know the answer," she said.

"Too bad, but I didn't really expect anything else." He sat down on the floor, in his lap his penis strutted proudly. "Come," he said. She accepted his invitation. Slowly she let him enter her again. Facing each other, they moved with deliberate slow motion.

How gentle he is, she thought when she looked into his dark eyes. *Too bad, we had to meet under these circumstances.* Her orgasms came at regular intervals, not earth shattering, but gentle, like their lovemaking.

After climaxing inside her, he dressed, went outside. When he came back, he carried two ration-packs, gave one to her. "I'm hungry," he explained. "Time for breakfast."

She ripped open the package, waited for a moment until the food inside finished expanding and heating itself. The smell of familiar food made her forget where she was. Sitting naked on one of the benches, she enjoyed a meal she thought she'd never have again. Commander Ko watched her and chuckled. "I can tell, you have been here for awhile."

She smiled. "This almost makes it worthwhile to be your prisoner."

"Only the food?" he asked.

"The food and the other thing, too." She laughed.

Ko walked up to the screen, moved his hand over it. Mirtin looked at the picture it displayed. She had seen the same room before.

A slim young woman knelt on the floor, her back arched, her small plump buttocks high. She reminded Mirtin a little of Vienne, except this woman had short black hair. Behind her, John Lambert pumped his lean buttocks with long, deep thrusts. Mirtin could actually see as his penis appeared and disappeared between the young woman's clenching buttocks.

"It seems Lambert is the interrogator, now," Mirtin murmured.

"It appears that way." Ko said.

The heavy breathing of Lambert and the woman came amplified over the speakers. "Oh...Ohh...I'm coming!" the female soldier cried out and Mirtin watched her buck underneath Lambert. Then she watched them change positions.

"He is quite skilled," Commander Ko observed.

"I wouldn't know," Mirtin mused, trying to remember what happened back in the Sanctuary. Nothing seemed really clear, they both had been intoxicated from the scent of those purple flowers and it had been over in a short time. "No," she said again, softly. "I wouldn't know."

She put down the empty pack, suddenly horny again. As if reading her mind, the commander met her in the middle of the room. He just pushed his pants down and moved behind her, then he made her bend down. She spread her legs, steadied herself against one of the swivel chairs. Feeling his thick warm penis between her thighs, she lifted her buttocks higher. He slid easily into her already dripping sheath.

Her eyes were glued to the screen. Watching Lambert and the woman, and listening to their ecstatic moans, heightened her own pleasure. Since Ko made no effort to turn off the screen, she suspected that watching the other couple affected him, also. His hard penis moved like a battering ram inside her inflamed vagina, steady and powerful. When he erupted inside her, she screamed. He put a hand over her mouth and told her with a gasping voice to keep it down.

Later he let her lie down on one of the benches again, to rest and recuperate, then he fucked her again. This time hard and without tenderness. He left her lying on the bench, sore and aching.

She closed her eyes, drifted into an uneasy slumber.

A weight on her chest woke her up. Opening her eyes, she looked into a grinning face. Then she became aware of a hard object moving inside her belly. She struggled to dislodge the man on top of her, but he was strong, kept her pinned down. Between her spread thighs his body moved with almost agonizing slowness. He didn't feel quite as big as Commander Ko, but close enough. His hands fondled her breasts, squeezed them until they hurt.

"Get that thing out of me!" she screamed. Then she saw the smiling face of Commander Ko. "Tell him to get off me!" she shouted angrily.

"I gave you a choice. You made the wrong one," he said, almost gently. Then he spoke to the soldier who was raping her. "The prisoner is all yours. She is nothing more than a whore."

"You bastard!" Mirtin screamed after him when he walked out of the exit. Then she saw the others, maybe four or five. They all had their pants down, waiting for their turn. The penis inside her jumped. She felt the hot discharge. When the man left her, two other soldiers grabbed her. They forced her onto her knees, buttocks up, held her while another one mounted her. He forced his pole into her, rode her for a long time. After a while, she was barely aware when one left and another took his place, but she knew that each one penetrated her several times.

Suddenly the door popped open. She heard the hissing sound of laser fire, saw bodies dropping to the ground. The man, who assaulted her, collapsed and rolled off her body. A gentle hand helped her up. She felt dizzy, her legs refused to obey. Someone picked her up, carried her into the open. It was daylight outside. She saw a familiar face above her.

"What did those bastards do to you?" Vienne sobbed. "Talk to me, Mirtin. Say you are alright."

"I'm fine. Now I am fine," she heard a croaking voice, realized it was her own.

Then she lost consciousness.

Chapter Twenty-one

"I know that you are still upset that we kept so much from you, but you would have done the same under the circumstances." Starmote's alien eyes were, as usual, unreadable. She smiled, but her smile was professional, without emotion.

She is an alien, not human, Beringer reminded himself. However, his attraction for her had not weakened. "I guess, it was naive of me to think you would trust us completely," Beringer said. "But if it makes you feel any better, I never trusted you either. I still don't." He closed his eyes and listened to the gentle sound of the waves slapping against the hull of the ship.

It wasn't a large ship, too small to brave the waves of the ocean, but large enough to sail this inland sea. The ship belonged to one of the sea-merchants who used it to transport people and goods from the *City of the Xandra* to the city at the north of the Great Lake. There were many, smaller settlements along the shores of the lake. All of them traded with the City.

Beringer went over the events that had transpired during these last two months.

The war-ship of the Mandarin Empire left the system. Admiral Tamoto reluctantly agreed to a temporary truce with the Genaar. The colonization of the southern continent by the one million Genaar settlers was well underway.

A treaty had been signed between the Xandra and Amaar after someone assassinated the Reverend, the self-anointed leader of the Pure-ones.

The problem with Numerika, the country to the west, still existed. Their leader, the Sergeant, refused to even talk with the representatives of the Xandra. The Great Mother had not asked for help in this matter from either Beringer or Starfinder. She felt confident that she could deal with the problem herself.

"My army will be ready soon," she told them. "Headed by my trusted General."

Beringer had met this *General*. He was the young savage Lambert rescued from certain death, the same man Sergeant Stasnowsky saved from the Naar. His name was Viran. His people lived on one of the big islands in the North Sea. They were considered barbarians by the inhabitants of the mainland.

A gentle hand touched Beringer's shoulder, and then a pair of soft lips kissed his mouth. Opening his eyes, he looked into the smiling face of Reyna. The Xandra-girl had delivered her baby and given it to the Great Mother to raise and care for. Actually, it had not been a baby…yet, just an egg, but Beringer could not bring himself to think of his child as an *egg*. Reyna had assured him that he was the father.

He looked into her lovely face. She seemed so young, so innocent, a girl just past puberty, but Beringer knew that her appearance was deceiving. Like all Xandra-born, she didn't age, not in looks. But in reality, she was near her *Time of Change.*

Soon her beautiful skin will begin to turn gray, he thought, *her flesh will shrink from her bones, her shiny hair will loose its black color and fall out. She will be craving meat and shun the light of day. She will become a Zomb.*

Beringer had been horrified when she told him, but she just laughed. "It is the way, Beringer."

He couldn't accept that. The Xandra called herself a goddess. Surely, she could do something. After all, she did restore the angel whose wings had been amputated by the Naar.

Looking into Reyna's beautiful green eyes, he promised himself to bring up the matter with the Xandra the moment they were back in the City. He reached up, pulled her face close to his and kissed her. She responded, and then she pulled away, smiling. "What was that for?" she asked.

"I just realized how much I love you," he said.

She put her hand against his cheek. "I love you, too, Beringer." She spoke softly, her face suddenly sad. "Soon I must leave you, but we still have some time together."

"We'll see," he said.

Reyna looked across the water, laughed and clapped her hands together. "Look," she said and pointed.

Beringer saw several heads appear on the water's surface. There was no ship or boat nearby and he wondered why anyone would swim so far away from shore. Slim arms parted the waves and the swimmers came closer with almost unbelievable speed.

Reyna waved to them and they waved back. Beringer caught glimpses of naked breasts as the swimmers turned onto their backs to look up at the people on the ship. He counted seven beautiful faces, framed by long black hair and seven pairs of breasts, full and round.

Laughing, the swimmers suddenly turned and disappeared under the surface. Before they were gone, seven broad fishtails slapped the water with noisy splashes.

"What are they?" Beringer asked.

"They are our sisters who live in the sea," Reyna explained.

"Amazing," Beringer said. "There are so many wondrous things in your world. A lifetime of studies will not be enough to unravel all the mysteries."

Chapter Twenty-two

My name is Stanislav Stasnowsky. I am a sergeant in the service of the Terran Space Navy.

At least I was a thousand years ago.

I still can't believe that nothing I left behind exists anymore. There is no more Terran Space Navy. My family and friends are gone. One thousand years gone.

And for me it has only been five years since we left the Solar System on board the Seed-ship.

Commander Beringer is trying to keep our unit together, but most of the soldiers have lost their sense of duty.

I know, I have.

There is nothing to fight for. We have no country, no ship. The space station belongs to an alien race. All the colonists on the planet we named Nu-Eden are long dead. Their descendants reverted to barbarism, and the other inhabitants may look human, but aren't.

We are strangers here and there is discontent among the men. They quarrel a lot. You don't have to be a psych to know at least part of the problem.

Women.

The Genaar-women are, without exception, very beautiful. But the Commander forbade us to start a relationship with them.

The irony is that he himself did not adhere to his own law.

I watched the holograms. I know what he did when he went on his mission to explore the planet Nu-Eden. The men know it, too. They are still stuck up there in the space station, all of them, except for Marine Cameron Sisko and me. He and I were among the team that rescued Lieutenant Wang and Lambert. Both of them are doing well and are also on the surface.

This is a strange place. Much that exists here defies scientific explanation, but I'm sure everything can somehow be explained.

Before Commander Beringer went down to the surface, we had a long talk. He confided in me that he didn't really trust the aliens, the Genaar, that they were keeping secrets from us.

I guess, he was right. We always thought that there were only about fifty of them on the station. That assumption turned out to be false. His suspicion was confirmed when they revived a hundred soldiers, most of them females, beautiful females. But their beauty is just another weapon. Apparently, none of them was born naturally.

They are designed fighting machines.

And then there are the one million colonists.

Just imagine, they were waiting for over two thousand years, frozen in the bowels of the station, waiting to be awakened.

They are being revived now and transported to the continent in the south, where the descendants of earlier Genaar settlers have been struggling to survive for two thousand years.

I've seen those descendants when we rescued Lieutenant Wang. They are not like the gentle Genaar I knew from the station. These people are fierce, ruthless killers. I guess that's what happens when every day is a fight for survival.

When I said there is nothing to fight for I was not quite truthful. Actually, there is. I've met this wonderful, most beautiful woman; and she is human. Her name is Mirtin. She is a soldier, but nothing like these Genaar-soldiers. Like I said, she is human.

She is the woman I rescued from the prison camp of the Mandarin Empire. We killed all of those bastards! After what they did to Mirtin, they deserved it. Mirtin has recovered, with help from that mysterious woman who calls herself the Xandra.

Mirtin and I hit it off and I think we might have a future together.

I may not be the most handsome guy around, not the smartest either, but I know how to treat a lady, and I would never cheat on her. And believe me, it is not an easy promise to keep, not after you've seen all those beautiful women running around everywhere, most of them scantily dressed, if at all.

There is only one problem with our relationship. She is a lieutenant with the Alliance, and she may have to honor her contract.

She has a ship hidden on one of the moons and is planning to return home. As part of her contract she has to take back the man, she was sent to rescue, a Colonel Massater, and deliver him safe and sound for debriefing. She will be gone for some time. But I can wait.

* * * *

Be sure to read the entire erotic Science Fiction Xandra Series.

www.ingramcontent.com/pod-product-compliance
Lightning Source LLC
Chambersburg PA
CBHW020131180626
46810CB00004B/1507